AN IRISH TALE
of a Modern Mystic

TANTRA MAAT

AN IRISh TALE
of a Modern Mystic
TANTRA MAAT

Distributed by:
Amazon: www.amazon.com
Barnes and Noble: http://www.barnesandnoble.com
Saturate Your Cells, the product division of METApoints,
the educational company of Tantra Maat, Inc.
http://store.saturateyourcells.com/

Edited by: Diane Covington
Cover illustration by: C Bean
Layout design by: Terrilyn Chance

Library of Congress Cataloging-in-Publication
Data has been applied for.
ISBN: 978-0-615-42283-1

creating reality through a language of unity
METApoints

ACKNOWLEDGEMENTS

There are so many people to thank. You know who you are. Without your generosity-- reading the drafts, jumping in and making sure the layout, the grammar and the icky, painstaking pieces were taken care of, this story could not have gone to press.

I want to acknowledge Diane Covington, my writing coach, teacher and the editor of this book, as well as my writing class…deep souls who, every Wednesday, travel to Diane's home to be silent and listen for the words to come.

I want to thank my children Liana and Aren for their unfailing love and commitment to have extraordinary lives.

I want to thank Glenn for his heroic determination to live a fulfilled life.

COVER ILLUSTRATION

Cindy "C" Bean

Growing up in SW Michigan, my first 10 years I was snuggled in a wooded corner alive with nature's spirits and guides.

During my first Ireland holiday in 1991, I was reunited with the nature spirits and spirit guides. From there 'we' began making their presence known through the colours of pencils and paints.

Currently living in SE Ohio and the Wayne National Forest amidst ancient Indian mounds and caves and the foothills of the Appalachians where the land is as alive as the Irish landscapes.

Living with 7 cats, 3 dogs and those that stop by for respite, food and healing, until their permanent homes are found.

My work for the past 34 years has been with young people and adults in mental and correctional institutions and foster care.

 I obtained a Bachelor of Fine Arts from The Columbus College of Art and Design, 1976, and a Master of Expressive Art Therapies from Lesley University, 1993

Primary Art Media – Oil, pastel, coloured pencil and graphite

THE PRELUDE

I close my eyes and I am transported to the shoreline of Dingle Bay on the western shore of Ireland. Stepping my bare feet into the ice-cold, black waters of the bay, my toes burrow into the gritty, black sand. With tears in my eyes, I say,

"Mother, I'm here."

She instantly responds. My feet become roots curling down into her core. A warm love flows up my legs pulsating with life in my torso. Symmetry of heart, mind, and soul floods me. I am ready to write.

There is no starting place for this tale, which is neither fact nor fiction. Whether the stories are based on illusion or truth, I leave to the heart of each reader.

But this is the true story of the transformation of a woman. I am that woman. I owe my transformation to the Irish, who won my heart and opened me to my soul; these stories are a tribute to them. The land of Ireland unrelentingly taught me what it is to truly be a member of this earth; this book is a tribute to it. The elementals and forces let me know undeniably that they are there; these stories are a tribute to them.

I came to Ireland an interloper. I left as a daughter. For that I am eternally grateful.

All was prepared for me the first day I landed. I was being 'minded' as they say in Ireland. The entirety of the journey unfolded for me over the next five years and set the stage for the journey to unfold for others.

The characters in this book are real people with real lives. They are modern heroes and heroines, who allow themselves to experience the full spectrum of living, from feeling like a buffoon to knowing themselves as part of the greatness of this Earth and its magic. I was graced to witness some of their struggles surfacing and to assist them to claim the 'magic' they carry and that they belong to.

Others are emissaries from the netherworlds that showed me undeniable evidence that there is more…so much more, and that it is so real.

Then there are the elementals, the primal forces, the gods and goddesses of the land and the sea that keep their dimensional worlds cocooned in the rock, earth and water.

I discovered the inexplicable quest of every human soul. Connected to the earth and her realms, we remember who and what we are. Modern fears fall away and in the presence of knowing one's true belonging, loneliness is banished. A spiritual reserve is always at hand to tap into during difficult times. We burst alive with humor. How could we have considered ourselves anything else?

There is one person whose name is not written in this book; yet she was my guide, my friend and my champion as I took on bringing this heartfelt and tender project into the world. She is my writing teacher and editor of this book, Diane Covington. Without her 'magic', this book would never have been written. When I go to writing class, the space is prepared. Every inch of her property with its apple and fig trees, deer, chickens and cats is touched by her and by the 'magic'.

When I sit down in her cozy front room, warmed by a blazing fire, or on her deck, warmed by the sun, I feel safe to write. In the intimacy of shared space with other developing writers, the land eagerly listens for our stories. Diane is the story of the land she shepherds and the land is the story of her heart. Her own life story, in its rawness and richness, creates a sanctuary for the exposure that everyone who writes must go through to get to their own unique gold. Thank you, Diane.

I will close this prelude with a story that embodies all the poets, writers, musicians and singers of Ireland. Without them the passionate wild hearts of human beings would not stay alive. Their music and prose stream out into the world, keeping alive our human stories…our vulnerability, and our grace. Listening to their words and their music feeds me and keeps me from drying up in the persistent emptiness of a western lifestyle.

Meeting the Muse

Cork Opera House circa 1992. Irish singer and Celtic Bard Mary Black's concert is sold out. I am so disappointed. After work I decide to walk past the opera house to see if I can hear her through the walls. I arrive just as the doors close.

A man is standing there. One lone man on an empty street except for the taxi man across the way with one lone taxi... my destination.

The man, dressed in a faded black business suit, walks toward me holding an umbrella in one hand and a performance ticket in the other. He holds the ticket high so I can see it. I gasp. Can it be? He puts the ticket in my hand and folds my fingers over it, clasping my hand in his. *"There's only one empty seat left in the house. It is yours."* He then releases my hand, tugs his cap in farewell and walks away.

I can't believe it. I rush to the door, terrified it will be locked, and determined to pound on it if necessary, until someone lets me in. The door opens without a hitch. Everyone is in their seats. There wasn't an usher in sight, but I can read the word 'balcony' on the ticket. Thank goodness. I race up the stairs. The rapture of the music shows in the faces as I enter. Sitting up straight, they lean forward in their seats, tapping their fingers and their feet to the music as it reverberates through the hall. I see one seat…my seat, first row balcony, right in the middle, looking straight down at Mary Black!

As the first song finishes, people rise to their feet shouting and applauding. I am shouting, crying, laughing, clapping, stomping, and wiping my nose, my eyes, my face… my hands squeezed periodically by the people on either side of me. Wave after wave of applause after each song builds an emotional power in the theater.

Mary Black announces the last song 'No Frontiers'. Everyone rises. Silence fills the theater. Without a word we all slip our arms around each others' backs. The orchestra plays to a standing audience, a thousand ogham stones of ancient memory.

Mary begins to sing.

We begin to sing with her.

Louder and louder the voices rise, singing the eulogy of all who have gone before.

As the first verse comes to an end, Mary stops singing. She lays her microphone down on the stage and stands, facing the audience …silent. The voices thunder. Each word reclaims us. Each stanza restores us.

As the last chorus begins, Mary picks up the microphone and sings with us.

"In your eyes faint as the singing of a lark

That somehow this black night

Feels warmer for the spark

Warmer for the spark

To hold us 'til the day when fear will lose its grip

And heaven has its way

And heaven has its way

When all will harmonise

And know what's in our hearts

The dream will realise

Heaven knows no frontiers

And I've seen heaven in your eyes

And I've seen heaven in your eyes"

BOOK ONE

THE CALL

"This is one race of people for whom psychoanalysis is of no use whatsoever."

—*Sigmund Freud (about the Irish)*

CHAPTER ONE

My Entrance into Ireland

Every day of my life, from my infancy to my early thirties, I was present to a part of me buried deep in my heart that wept for lost worlds. No one could hear my cry... not even when the stethoscope would rudely press against my breast listening for a beat. Not even then.

You see, no instrument of man can pick up the vast strength of the unseen worlds that lies in the flesh and soul of every human being. My silent cry lived where the muscles of the heart pressed so tightly against each other that no sound could be heard. Every person, whether or not they realize it, carries that cry. I could never shut it out.

It took a small island nestled between the northern route of the Gulf Stream and the British Isles to reach the depth of me and restore my soul. And over time, I took others back so that they, too, could rediscover their 'torn away worlds'.

When I went to Ireland for the first time, I did not know that I was embarking on a journey that would transform my life on all levels. I did not know that I would uncover lost gifts. People tell wonderful stories about how going to Ireland is like going to heaven. My first trip to Ireland, however, did not occur like heaven.

First of all, I went at almost the worst time of year, in January 1989. I found out later, only February would have been worse. The world of this small island in the winter is dark, dreary, damp, and muggy all at the same time.

I had never thought of going to Ireland. I had never wanted to go to Ireland. And even worse, I thought that all of Ireland was in a violent revolt against the British. I had no idea there was a Northern Ireland and a Southern Ireland. I knew nothing about Ireland except maybe the song "When Irish Eyes are Smiling."

I was married at the time. And God bless my children. They always knew I wasn't 'normal'. My husband treated me like I was normal though, and was usually offended by the 'abnormal behavior' I exhibited in the face of so many of what he called 'normal things'.

At that time, I did (and still do) psychic consultations. What the United States of America calls psychic is actually fortunetelling, which means predicting your future. In Europe, they understand more deeply what psychic means. The word comes from psyche, the mind of your soul. Psychics, if true to their name, tell you who you are, what you are connected to, and what is in and out of alignment in your life, all based on being present to the sweet mystery of your soul.

In the late 80's, I was bored. While I adored my children, I was not cut out for the routine of every day suburban existence. I needed my soul fed and could not find what I needed anywhere. So because I was bored, I offered to do a two-for-one consultation. Two consultations for the price of one would be auctioned off at a neighborhood fair that my children's friends' parents (the 'normal' suburban people) thought was so much fun.

I was a recluse back then, and didn't go to the fair. I found out through a phone call that a pair of Jeans, two ladies who had only been roommates for about five days, had bought the consultations.

I had no idea that 'Irish Jean' and 'Columbus, Ohio Jean' would forever change the course of my life. 'Columbus, Ohio Jean' is another tale. My entrance into the world of Ireland began with 'Irish Jean' who had worked in Dublin and was intent upon my doing consults there. She only knew one person in Dublin, Lainey, who still lives there, and to this day is still my client.

Lainey found a spiritual center where I could do consults and off I went, bag, tape recorder, and cassette tapes in hand. I headed for a strange country, to meet a woman I had never met.

When I arrived, I was greeted by a man named Brendan. Brendan looked more like a sailor than the head of The Irish Spiritual Life Centre in Dublin, Ireland and their main psychic. It turned out he had been a sailor and had 'manned' a lighthouse for over 25 years. Brendan, his young wife, and their three kids had all come to Dublin because a vision told him to leave the coast and the lighthouse and surrender to a higher will.

SOOOOOO! Here I was, overweight, loaded down, ignorant, and very nervous, being shown up the narrow stairway to my 'reading room'. Hauling my large butt up three stories worth of extremely narrow stairs, I thought a few times that I was going to be wedged between the walls. What a candidate for humor!

I reached the top of the stairs and surveyed my room. Even as I hung onto the doorframe, gasping for breath, the room made the climb worth it. It was simple yet endearing, with windows overlooking the rooftops of Dublin. Small and a bit barren, it had two chairs and a table for consults, but with handmade curtains that added a homey touch. A slight whistle blew through the closed windows that lined three of the walls, creating the feeling that one might still be on the coast manning a lighthouse after all.

As I stepped into the room, the wooden floor creaked and the floorboards gave in a bit, reminding me of the proximity of the floors underneath if the floor gave way. But I felt a comfort in the isolation of this room away from the rest of the Centre. I loved my own workplace in the strange land I could barely see for the drizzling rain outside.

Leaving the Centre the first day with Lainey, we drove down the fog-laden, austere coastline to Sandymount, Ireland and the B&B where I would be staying. The house, large for an Irish home, was built along the coast road. I could hear the lapping of waves in the gray dusk of evening and could smell the salt mixed with drizzle in the air. I slunk out of the car and headed for the door of the B&B. While I still could not see my hand in front of my face, I sensed that the view would be gorgeous if it ever stopped raining.

I was drenched. Jet lag was pulling me down. I could feel my eyes drooping and a fatigue filling my body with such force that I suddenly needed to lie down.

Somehow on cue, I was met at the door by a kind landlady with a glass of Black Bush, the guardian who protects you so you can survive the Irish winters. Black Bush is made by Bushmills, and is *"an Irish whiskey made to rival any other whiskey for many a whiskey drinking man,"* so she reported with a smile.

Lainey left, having deposited her charge. I was immediately whisked into my bed, a hot water bottle placed under my feet, and Black Bush unspoiled by water or soda on my nightstand. Back then, there was no heat during the night in Ireland. Exhausted, my chest afire with whiskey, my bladder waiting to explode, I forced my mind over my matter, and slept until dawn.

The next day, I would begin my work in this strange land. I walked out the door and made my way to the train that would take me between my B&B and the Centre. The 'rail', as the Irish call it, stretches up the eastern coastline between Sandymount and Dublin.

By the third day, I had a cold setting up housekeeping right in the center of my chest. Yet, it was truly staved off from being anything worse by the nursing of my B&B landlady, Mrs. Brady. She was ready every night when I came back with whiskey and a water bottle in hand.

Ireland is damp. That is the one thing you can say about Ireland without being wrong at any moment in time. Everything was damp back in the 80's. Ireland was considered a third world country until the influx of the Euro in the late 90's. The peat fires, which burned in Mrs. Brady's hearth back then, helped some, but not a lot. Each morning, I dreaded putting my feet onto the cold floor, and pulling my body out of the warmth of my cozy bed and into the shock of icy air.

I would gasp my way through a dripping shower to be greeted by a breakfast where my belly would be rewarded with pork sausage and rashers, the Irish word for bacon. No matter what we think about pork in our diet, in Ireland it is a godsend for those of us who prefer to be warm in damp weather. For me, that Irish breakfast was a joy to behold. Eggs, oatmeal, bread, orange juice, and stout Irish tea were included in the morning menu. Also included was black and white blood pudding. When I found out that it was made from the reproductive organs of a pig, I politely declined.

I loved traveling the 'rail'. Moving into the train, I was greeted by a steady stream of lilting voices laughing, wittily discussing their workday, their family matters, or just plain talking for the sake of companionship and camaraderie. They laughed and joked with one another. Never once was I shoved aside by a 'suit' racing to get to his corporate office. I was amazed how they never seemed to be swayed by beauty or appearance. Everyone was treated the same, no matter what they looked like. They seemed to see right to the heart of a person.

On one particularly busy day, an American family was boarding the train. There are no porters on Irish trains. The rail was a rustic version of a New York subway. The cars pulled up to the station. The doors opened. An unspoken movement on and off began, all in a light-footed, graceful dance.

The American parents and their two grammar school children were clearly braced for the madness of the subway. The doors opened. The Irish simply grabbed the suitcases and the two children while pressing gently into the backs of the parents to accompany them through the doors. The woman, trying to recover from a sudden momentary loss of her children, was reunited with them as the children were jovially swung up in the air and plopped on the floor beside her.

The father bristled and rushed for the suitcases that were gingerly making their way ahead of him. As he reached to grab one of the two men who he clearly thought were thieves, the men stopped and without a signal, people on the train bench cleared out, making room for these newcomers to their land. The shaken mother and father were shown a seat. The confused children were smiled at and patted on the head. The suitcases were put up on top and the self-appointed valets tipped their hats to the family, wishing them a good day. It took time for the visitors to recover from such benevolent hospitality.

I found out early on, that in the brisk wind that roars across the sea between England and Ireland, an umbrella was a joke. The Irish seem to be weather immune. Simple knee-length wool coats and a scarf were the attire of the day. Later, I would watch as a modern economy rose with the influx of new money and 'shop-till-you-drop' would flood the once easygoing attitude of the Irish people.

But in the beginning, I was privileged to be one of the people there before the modern world infiltrated the shores of Éire, the Irish word for Ireland. Yet even in the modern times that would come, you could still feel the gods and goddesses of Éire, watching and caring for their people and their land.

Ireland totally enveloped me. I came with three days of scheduled consults. By the end of the second day, they had three weeks of appointments scheduled for me.

What a mix! On one hand, I was sure I was not going to survive the damp dreary weather. On the other, I was enthralled with the souls of the Irish, both on the streets and in the consult room.

"In dreams begin responsibilities."

—*William Butler Yeats*

chapter two

It Begins

*M*y bedroom in my B&B had changed. When I went to bed earlier that night, the room was painted white. I was tucked up in a single bed against a small window that was out of the way of the wind. The radiator, which of course was never on, was within reach. When I awoke in the middle of the night, I was groggy, but even groggy I could remember what the room I was staying in looked like.

The bed was now in the middle of the room, or perhaps I should say 'a' room. I felt drugged and two-minded. One mind was thinking simple thoughts like, 'Oh, this is a dream and even though it seems real, I will wake up soon'. The other mind was busy adjusting to 'NEVER NEVER Land'!

Through the sluggish haze, I noticed that my bright, sunny room with the flowering wallpaper was now not bright at all. In fact, as I tilted my head up from my pillow, the room faded away into black space. This unnerved me.

Still clinging to the 'I am in a dream' thought, I began to notice that my cover was no longer the white and posy-covered duvet it had been. Instead, I was covered with a thick white fog that was streaming toward a door that had become part of my room from God knows where. As I became more awake, the tug of the menacing mist--at least it occurred as menacing at the time--was sucking into me more and more. I was being dragged out of my bed toward an awaiting door!

Do not ask me what foolishness enters the edges of our thoughts when confronted with the unbelievable. All I know is that I knew to turn over. But it wasn't quite as simple as that. I stiffened into a frantic state of 'OH! MY GOD!' and threw myself over, gripped my arms under me, and curled up in a yoga pose for pregnant women! Face down, hiding from what I did not know. Everything changed again, and I suddenly felt like I was back in the bed I had gone to sleep in earlier.

The sweat under my arms reminded me that I was terrified. My 'right' room was twice as small as the chamber I had just been in a second ago -- a dark, dank, hypnotic, and commanding chamber. I was beyond dumbfounded or stupefied. I was beyond thunderstruck or loopy. I was consumed by a haunting memory that I could not get to the foreground of my thoughts. I had no idea what had happened.

While strange and definitely terrifying, the event reminded me of another world that I had somehow forgotten.

I was clear that the fog had come for me. I knew that it

knew me and that I knew it as well. I entered a dissociative state of confusion. There was the 'me' who had come to Ireland to work, going through the paces of doing consults, while another 'me' began to remember. The two 'me's' were not very compatible and seemed to have no way to come together. So, I got up, dressed... and went to breakfast.

Preoccupied by my two-world feeling, it took me a minute to realize that I was playing with my food, making patterns in the eggs, and neatly arranging the rashers into an odd geometric design. When I looked up, I realized that my landlady was staring at me. I started to apologize, but the words stopped in my throat. She was smiling!

"What on earth can she be smiling about?" I thought. The worst part was, that as I thought that thought, I knew somewhere in the back of my brain what she was smiling about. *"Damn, I wish I could remember. What did I know that I couldn't remember?"* Whatever it was, I saw it in her eyes. But I still couldn't remember.

She never stopped smiling and staring at me, as I, as normally as possible, bolted for my bedroom to dress as fast as I could and get the hell out of there.

Tucked safely on the train to work, the absurdity of the experience moved in, and I relaxed into the common remedy for these kinds of adventures. I chalked it up to my imagination. The day went quite well. I made it up the three flights of stairs, only stopping about ten times instead of twenty. There's nothing like adrenalin to get the body moving.

I loved reading the Irish psyche. Their cells had not forgotten.

When I was with them, their cells were alive with the memory of ancient rituals, codes of honor, powerful magi, and awesome warriors. Worlds that I had known about from the day my baby mind formed its first thought. When I read the Irish, I tumbled back into the sweet juice of remembering. I felt refreshed.

I am a cellular empath. What is that? Well, I'll try to explain. You see, there is something we all have forgotten, just like I forgot in my bedroom that morning. When I do a consult, people begin to remember. It is a powerful and intimate experience.

Confronting paranormal phenomena is a training of self-discovery. I have been a student of phenomena pretty much since I was a small child. My first memory of the paranormal was when I was eight months old and I melded with the mind of a cow. Ireland was to be my 'no college needed' graduate degree in the paranormal. Once you remember who you really are, there is no going back.

I was anxious at the end of the day when I was headed back to the B&B. I feared it might be, at bare minimum, the near equivalent to a witch's coven. Gathering my courage, standing up straight, I opened the door to the house that barred itself daily from the fierce winds of the Irish Sea. I turned around and realized that the Eye of Howth, a rock formation directly in the waters opposite the house, was aligned with the sun as it set in the evening. Another clue… to what I didn't know, nor was I eager to find out.

Entering the house, I saw the Irish whiskey waiting for me. Was it laced with hallucinogens? I wasn't sure.

" Touch can mean distance to some people
Touch can mean prison or be like a cage
I always thought that life could be more simple
Specially in this day and age. "

'Babes in The Wood'
—Mary Black

CHAPTER THREE

Meeting Mod

I t took me a few years to realize that the Irish are extremely polite, almost to a fault. If you live with them awhile,
however, you can tell when they are insulting someone to
the bone. It is amazing because the other person barely real-
izes they are being insulted. Reflecting back on those first
few weeks in Ireland, I didn't know if Mrs. Brady was being
polite or 'slagging' me – the Irish form of disrespect.

She never mentioned that I stopped drinking the Irish
whiskey. Irish B&B's have a dining room that can fit about
five small tables. 'We', the guests, lived upstairs and down
a small hallway and the 'family' lived in the back on the

ground floor. In this case, the family was only Mrs. Brady, and being off-season, I was the only guest. Every morning at breakfast I would sit at my same table. I sat facing the window that looked out on the sea. I could see the edge of the Eye of Howth through the white lace curtains that brightened the dullness of the Irish winter outside.

She used her fine china, including those dainty teacups that barely wet one's palate. The flowers were fresh. Since she never seemed to leave the house, I always wondered where she got them.

A few days after the incident in my bedroom, I was finally relaxing a bit. No new incidents had occurred, so my theory that she was spiking my whiskey grew in proportion to my relief. I had the day off, and I was looking forward to a walk along the Irish Sea and a long afternoon nap.

It was early morning, so when the telephone, that never rang, rang, I was startled and jumped up from my chair, jostling the fine china. The jangling of dishes stayed in the air, summoning Mrs. Brady, who seemed oblivious to the ringing phone. I was standing, staring down at the phone and watching it ring, wondering if it was for me. I looked up at her as she looked at the dishes, then at me, and finally at the phone. The wonder was that the phone kept ringing.

One of the valuable aspects of no answering machine is that the phone will not go to voicemail. One of the problems is that you will not know who called unless you answer it. Clearly, this was a problem we shared. The persisting phone finally irritated her enough that she answered. She listened for what seemed like a long time, then laid the phone down on the table and turned to leave. Halfway across the living room, she turned, looked at me, and said, *"It's for you."* One of the things I have learned through being in Ireland is to never be offended.

Of course, in my psychic way, I knew it was for me, but psychics doubt, too. I picked up the black heavy phone that I had watched in every black and white movie when I was young and seen on every Ma Bell commercial. I was sure the party on the other end of the line had hung up. I put the phone to my ear and said, *"Hello?..."*

A gravelly, coarse voice struck out at my eardrum, *"This is Mod. Brendan told me about you."* ('You' was spoken like a stern grade school teacher pointing her finger at you, elongated to make that perfect effect of shrinking you into your proper place.) *"I will be by in exactly twenty-two minutes to pick you up and take you to Glendalough."* With that pronouncement, there was only the dial tone left in my very puzzled ear.

I got ready. There was no calling Brendan to see who this strange voice was that was picking me up in a very few minutes. The Centre had no phone. People called Brendan's home, and his wife scheduled them for appointments. Old times still had their ways here. Mrs. Brady called up, *"There is a car outside waiting for you."* I went down the stairs, booted, and encased in a windbreaker, ready for just about anything... except for what I saw.

I opened the door. In front of me was an elderly woman with a gnarled body that looked as if it had intertwined itself with the earth. Birds could have nested in her tangled disheveled hair. She wore at least two dresses. The top dress was worn thin, revealing the bits and pieces of one or more underneath. She looked completely out of place standing on the sidewalk leading up to the B&B. I found myself yearning to return her to the woods where she could entwine herself with the rest of nature. Even her mismatched dresses carried the ambiance of weeds and flowers all jumbled up together. Her rolled down men's socks and high mud stained brown boots that I suspect were men's too, grabbed her legs like the roots of a tree straining to push down into the ground. Her hands were gardening hands, with dirt still under her nails. She grabbed the hem of my jacket and pulled me toward her car.

Her car! What a joke! Her car was a Volkswagen shell that must have been picked up at some burn site. There was not an ounce of paint on it. The seats were covered with aged cloth that matched her clothing, like some kind of surrealistic art project. The seats were okay, just WAY past their prime. The floor exposed the car's bare, steel gray metal frame. Tufts of rotted carpet clung to the rusted metal, looking like they were holding on for dear life.

The incident in my Irish bedroom loomed up at me. The feeling that somehow this was an extension of that moment enhanced the supernatural impact of simply getting into the car. *"Oh! My! What is happening to me?"* was my last conscious thought as my female munchkin driver held the revving starter until the rusty bucket of metal lurched into gear.

I did not know where Glendalough was or what it was. I

just knew we were going there. Mod began to talk as soon as we both got into the car. After a minute or two, I began to put the pieces together. She was telling me that scientists from a country I had never heard of had come to find plants that could be used in some kind of medicinal healing. She went on about how she had taken some medium-sized rocks out of her garden, down to the sea near where she lived and laid them gently at the edge of the shore, the water barely covering them.

As she spoke of these things, her demeanor changed. What emerged was a spry old woman whose wisdom surpassed the most knowledgeable people on the planet. She was connected in. She was beautiful. She glowed. I could see her rocks with my inner eyes and her love for them. I could see the sea washing over them until they gave up their secrets to this woman they loved as much as she loved them. While I was so present to this mystery before me, she was explaining how she told the scientists what the rocks had told her--where they could find the plants.

Before I could digest this thoroughly, she screamed, turning back into an old hag, *"Pay attention! We have to get this car up this hill!"* I looked out and realized that while the car was definitely running, it was clearly not going uphill. In fact, it was beginning to move backwards. *"Think! Think it up the hill,"* she screamed. *"What kind of *#^%! psychic are you, anyway?!"*

Well, I will tell you. I began to think that car up that hill with all my might. Soon, the backward drift stopped and the wheels miraculously moved the car forward. Not a word was spoken, the concentration level was so strong, until we got to the top of the hill and the car could coast down the other side in neutral.

"What motion of the sun or stream or eyelid shot the gleam that pierced my body through? What made me live like these that seem Self-born, born anew?"

'Stream and Sun at Glendalough'
—William Butler Yeats

chapter four

Glendalough
PART I: The Vikings

The wildness in Ireland carries true symmetry. As we drove along that day, I could see the remnants of the Irish gods and goddesses in so many places. They were in how the oak and the holly trees positioned themselves, preserving the ancient holiness that extends beyond the scope of modern man. They were in the nipple tipped mountains that called on the sky and in the moist brindled mosses that carved out secret hideaways amidst the jagged rocks covering the landscape. I would always be caught by the aliveness of Ireland. Every bush, every flower, every tree, every rock carried the signature of the god or goddess that created it.

The spiritual creativity brought into being a living dynamic that expressed an inviting secrecy.

They say in Ireland that everyone is Irish. There is some truth in that. Ireland captures the deepest part of you that lives in unity with all things. It hears the whispers, *"Come back to me. Let me hold you. Let me bring you back to life, with all the wondrous meanings that live without need for words. Let me soak your cells, satisfy and nourish your depths, so that you are never the same."*

The cells vibrate awake… drowsy maybe, and perhaps not quite able to focus on what is truly there in the beginning. It doesn't matter. You are captured. The land is alive, and you become alive in a primal silence.

Devas are the beings that live cocooned in the land of Ireland. They care take the land and conceal themselves from view, but their magic affects you. You have heard of the faeries and the leprechauns. There are many, many more! I had, at the time of Mod and Mrs. Brady, just barely been introduced to this magic. I had no real comprehension of what that magic would mean to my life in the years to come.

As we rolled down the winding road toward Glendalough, the ancientness of Ireland glowed all around me in the greens of the moist land, the sparkling blue streams cascading under the road down into the steep valley, and the brown lush earth that complimented scene after scene. It took my breath away.

Glendalough is the valley of enchantment. We had driven through miles and miles of country, barren of trees and yet alive with the peat that preserves the bodies, the villages, and the roads that once existed there. I could see the places where peat had been cut and stacked to dry. Mrs. Brady had burned a peat fire every night in the fireplace. The smell of peat takes you back to your primordial roots. You want its smell. It's a subtle reminder of the swamp we once dragged ourselves out of, when still a simple and not yet multifaceted organism.

Leaving the barren peat landscape, we plunged into deep valleys of waterfalls and green. Ireland is famous for its green--I would call it a celebratory green-- everything looks like it is celebrating! The journey up, down, and around the winding road consisted of shouts from Mod to concentrate on getting the car (that seemed to love to go backwards) up and over the numerous hills we encountered.

At the bottom of one hill, a modern stop sign surprised me. There it was in the middle of nowhere right in front of us on the right side of the road. When I saw that sign I had to shake off a feeling of loss. Once again, I found the ancient mystery of Ireland much more fulfilling than the modern sites set aside for tourists.

We turned right into an Irish tourist spot to use the facilities. There was the big parking lot for the buses, with the Tourist Information Centre faithfully built beside it. Even with this modern setting, the trees rose up behind, hugging the mountain with their splendor. My eye caught a shape cut into the ground beside the cars. I asked Mod what it was. *"It is a labyrinth, of course,"* she replied. *"Of course"*, I thought, *"Silly me!"* In Ireland, there would be a labyrinth next to a modern parking lot.

We drove past the tourist venue and past an old hotel. I would, over the years, stay at the steadfast Glendalough Inn many, many times. We crossed over a roaring creek and made our way on a level patch of road, thank goodness, winding between high banks lined with bushes on either side.

In Ireland, the old Irish roads take two cars where roads that size would barely take one car in the United States. My first time I rode with an Irish driver, I was clear that the Irish were definitely psychic. A taxi driver offered to show me around the outskirts of Dublin. My Irish driver rounded the curves at a high rate of speed that day, suddenly slamming on the brakes as he met another car on the road. He pressed tight up against the bushes as the other car zoomed by. Then my driver whipped back out, no pause needed... all as natural as natural could be.

Over the years, rarely did I see a car wreck, yet how two cars passed on Irish roads was quite beyond me.

I could see the upper and lower lakes of Glendalough. An old, single tower came into view. This was where, long ago, the priests had hidden from marauders, mostly Vikings. An occasional double world started up. I would get glimpses of men in hides and metal horned helmets running through the trees. Then, when I looked again, they were gone.

The next minute I would be watching Mod drive. She drove at a level of concentration that was frightening. I couldn't help wonder if she needed to concentrate that much to stay on the road.

We squealed into a smaller parking lot with fewer cars.

Without a word, we got out and began to walk toward the ruins of an old chapel. Now the glimpses were becoming full-blown experiences. I could hear fierce yelling coming down through the trees to the right of me. Then, when I looked again nothing was there.

I followed behind Mod who, regardless of her age, was moving like an athlete. We got to an area of flat ground, with a lake on one side of us and a chapel on the other. At that moment, I collapsed into the ground. I curled up, holding my knees against my chest, scared I was going to be sick and at the same time glad I had worn pants. I had changed worlds again.

I was lying on the ground feeling the vibration of a horde of pounding feet coming over the tall ridges that lined the valley floor. I heard, felt, and saw monks pouring out of the dwellings by the side of the lake. I saw the monks harvesting in the fields drop their spades and run. I knew they had no place to run. I groaned in anguish as the first Viking plunged his ax into the back of a young monk who had tripped on his habit and lay sobbing on the ground.

Shouting, I had to describe everything going on around me. It was the only relief I had for the anguish of the souls I felt.

Sobbing, I reached for the hand of a small child whose body was crushed by the marauders spilling into the village around the monastery. The mother lay dead beside her, the look of horror frozen on her face. Other images caught my eye as I saw the Vikings slaughtering the village men, corralling the women and dragging them off to rape them.

I vaguely heard, *"Is she okay?"* and *"What's wrong with her?"* coming from the local time around me, but the constant barrage of images that moved through me and around me obliterated any semblance of stability.

I was caught in the horrendous event of a day long gone. I felt the earth trembling from the weight of the men around me. Even with my eyes closed, the smells of cattle, turned up earth, and fresh lake water mixed with dust in the air were pungent ... far beyond imagination.

The Vikings killed and pillaged all around me. Older monks covered the bodies of younger monks, hoping that if they survived, the legacy of the Christian God would carry on. Goats and pigs were driven out of holding pens, across the strip of ground between the lakes where I was curled up. Women and children were being herded up the valley. I saw, behind my closed eyes, the feet of the pigs and goats as they scurried away in the face of the shouts around them.

I watched as the Vikings left some monks and villagers living so they could rebuild the monastery and village, so in a few years the Vikings could come and pillage and slaughter again. Rivers of blood soaked the fields. Invading intentionally at harvest time, the Vikings had stripped all the gardens of their produce, leaving the monks and villagers in jeopardy as they entered the winter season.

Usually a monk would keep watch in a tall skinny tower at the open entrance to the valley. He would warn everyone, then climb up and pull up the ladder so no one could enter. The monk in the tower had not seen them coming that day.

This time the Vikings had poured down into the deep valley from the top of a mountain ridge at the far end of the lake. To this day that ridge is nearly impossible to climb up or come down. The slate and limestone scatter your feet. That day, the Vikings hadn't cared. Thirsting for surprise, they had skidded and rolled and slipped down the mountain, screaming their hostility and violence into the quiet afternoon air. They were a herd of raging beasts roaring down through the forests, surrounding the lakes, destroying peaceful lives with their savage ways.

Back in 'real' time, I was surrounded by a crowd of tourists and locals. Mod was translating everything I was experiencing. She was the wisdom teacher sharing with the people the history of this valley before the raids ended and peace was won.

I was the living demonstration Mod needed to awaken the people again to the land. She seemed completely unconcerned that I was drooling at the mouth with tears streaming down my face and that my body was twitching uncontrollably, traumatized by what I saw.

"Come away, O human child!
To the waters and the wild
With a faery, hand in hand,
For the world's more full of weeping
than you can understand."

'The Stolen Child'
—William Butler Yeats

CHAPTER FIVE

Glendalough
PART II: The Faery

Though a strong overbearing energy held me to the ground, I tried to get to my knees. Dizzy, I put my hands on the ground. I made it half way up, head hanging, fearing I would vomit.

I could hear Mod kindly asking the people to leave us now. The world was still spinning. As where I was in real time returned, the sounds around me were still mixed with screams and the smell of blood and feces, from the terror and fear of the dying monks and villagers. The force of the experience bore weight over everything around me.

Mod changed again. Shifting from her attention on the people, she turned her full attention on me. Sitting down beside me, she rolled me over on my side and held my head in her lap. She stroked my head as I wept. I remember thinking, "I had no idea how gruesome life could be." But, mostly, I was relieved that I was getting a break from the images that had been assaulting my mind, threatening to fragment my sanity. I realized that Mod's crooning and rocking was pushing the images out of my mind. As she cuddled me like a small child, the images, sounds, and smells suddenly stopped.

The few people that were left around us helped me to sit up. New people who had heard about what had happened had gathered. There was such generous concern and caring on all the faces. One little boy about four years old with a blue short panted suit on came up and leaned over and stroked my face. That did it! I started sobbing all over again.

I heard Mod saying, *"She is from America. She is a well-known mystic who is experiencing what happened on this land."*

Over the years, I have realized that when you are called to be what you have come to be, you don't think about how people might perceive you. I did not realize when I came to Ireland that I carried the reputation of a fairly famous psychic from the United States of America.

I appreciated Mod's words. I realized that I was very self-conscious sitting on the ground, my nose running with my eyes swollen. I expected me to at least have my s____ together. I felt publicly embarrassed, and yet no one but me seemed to care. This public embarrassment would persist throughout the years I came to Ireland until finally all semblance of concern for how I appeared, disappeared. I could simply be present to what I was present to and share that with whoever else was there.

Mod, donning her wisdom hat again, explained to our new visitors that in the 1400's, the monks and the villagers who lived around the monasteries to worship were fair game for the Vikings. They would wait until areas were developed and then come in and rape, pillage, and destroy. People lived in constant fear.

I sat up while Mod was talking and was listening to her explain what I had seen. I remember thinking how strange it was that I could at one moment be in a totally different experience and the next minute be back in the present. I was listening to a history lesson that Mod had shared before like a teacher with her students.

Later, I would learn that this is the way of it when you begin to open up to the great landscape of creation. One minute you are in the presence of something horrible or something sublime. The next minute, it is over, and you shift into dishes and shopping. Without the emotional realm of a human being being mature and strong, one small mystical event can set you off for a week. This was far more than a small event.

People helped me to my feet and, with the reverence that is ingrained in the Irish soul, left to let us be.

Mod took my hand and, without a word, began walking toward the path by the lake where the Vikings had entered. When I stood up and looked out on the lake, trying to avoid the sight of the monastery ruins on the left, I saw the waterfalls that fed the lake at the far end. White water slivered the black rock into five or six streams that slid over each other, tumbled with each other, beckoning the sun to join them. Responding, the sunlight hit the glistening rock sending streaks of light out over the lake. Tall swaying evergreens stood majestically on either side, silent witnesses.

Mod and I started our trek toward the modern concrete path that led by the lake. Before we got to the path that lead to the waterfalls, she stopped and so did I, still not too sure footed after my ordeal.

I began to hear singing. Soft singing that had a high pitched almost birdlike sound to it. The sound was clearly, however, the voice of a young woman's. A very small young woman, I would discover! Mod watched as I followed the sound. It was coming from a hole in the bank of the lake. Ferns and moss partially hid the hole. A tiny rivulet ran out into the lake.

Then I saw her. A small winged girl was singing with joy and love. Her hands reverently reached out toward a small twig with an infinitesimally tiny leaf on it. Her small body was covered with a water-made translucent film. She was no more than 3 inches tall. She was a faery.

Then she was no more. I was simply looking at a small strip of clear water coming out of a hole in the bank. No glistening ferns or inviting moss. No small creature delicately bringing all of her tiny voice to bear in celebrating the news of the new leaf on the small twig before me. The leaf had returned to its insignificant status in the human world. I stood there a long time.

I never said a word to Mod. But… I knew she was pleased. Humbled before such mystery, I took Mod's hand, and we started on the path toward the waterfall.

"I'm what you humans call a leprechaun, and my study is humans," he commenced.

'Summer with the Leprechauns'
—Tanis Helliwell, M. Ed.

chapter six

Glendalough
PART III: The Leprechauns

It was nice just to be walking with nothing out of the ordinary happening. We dropped hands after awhile and Mod left me to explore the shoreline, talking with rocks, birds, and whatever else she was relating to. I ambled along the path, drinking in the light sliding between the trees, casting silhouettes everywhere.

Mod joined me as I got to the end of the path. Thank goodness! The path stopped, blocked by gigantic rocks.

Mod knew her way through. We climbed deftly over the boulders until we got to the other side. What a site! The ruins of late 1800's buildings had once been rock houses with thatched roofs. No indoor plumbing, I assure you. Many of the ruins sat in shallow water. We walked on the stone slabs lying on the ground to make our way around them. It was all that was left of a quarry that mined the granite rocks of the glacial valley for quartz veins of silver, lead and zinc. The quartz crystals glistened everywhere I looked.

I wanted to stay and saturate myself with the energy of the valley bottom. It was clearly the heart of The Mother. A womblike, fertile energy embraced me. I could feel the heartbeat of The Mother, vibrating life in this area enveloped by black rock and roaring water. I had never felt the pulse of the earth before. I hollered at Mod to ask her what it was.

"You are standing on a huge vortex that reaches all the way down to the core of The Mother. What happened here hurt The Mother's heart," she answered.

I sat down with a heavy heart. For years, I would hear of The Mother. I would develop a course about women, which returned them to the heart of The Mother. And yet, it would be a long time before The Mother would reveal her far-reaching mystery to me.

The power of a mystery is that you can never fully understand it. You only experience it. This is the joy of heaven on earth. I let myself be held by this energy. I never wanted to leave. But I either followed Mod, or I was left stranded in the middle of nowhere. Given my blissful disoriented state,

I would never find my way out. I call it being 'dimensionally challenged'.

So off we went, my very overweight body hauling itself over one boulder after another until I was exhausted. Thank the Lord we returned to the path on the other side of the mine site. Over the years, this path and its side paths would become more than familiar to me and I, an adopted Irish, would help new Ireland initiates through this labyrinth of stone.

I finally sat down to rest on the nearest rock that would accommodate my substantial tush. I was breathing heavily. Though I never stopped going where I wanted to go, I really did drag my body along. My ankles and hips often screamed in agony. So I sat, relieved to be out of the fray of the energy that had assaulted me upon arrival to Glendalough.

I sat on the rock for a moment, admiring the close up view of the waterfalls. I was thinking that we should never trust our perception. The water looked one way from across the lake and up close it looked totally different. Now the water was clear, gushing up and over the rocks. The wall of rock was a waterslide of rapids hurtling down into the ground, becoming streams that fed the lake.

Mod had walked up to the top of the hill ahead of me, and was on the ground searching for something with her fingers. *Then something dropped on my head.* This was curious because there was only sky above me.

"It must be a bird," I thought.

I felt on my head and pulled a small piece of mica from my

hair. As I sat there looking at it, appreciating its sparkle and makeup, another one hit the top of my head. I was flabbergasted. There was nothing around – absolutely nothing. *Then it happened again, and again.*

Then it began to rain mica. I put my hands on top of my head to protect it from the sharp pricks of mica that hit sideways on my crown. I looked up at Mod, and she was staring, clearly as surprised as I was. Then she screamed, "RUN!" I ran. I huffed and puffed as fast as I could up the path until I got to her, my head full of mica. I crumpled on the rock near where Mod was standing as she shouted at the rocks and the sky in Gaelic.

The power of all that I had experienced since I had been in Ireland came crashing down on me, and I, yet again, wept. Then the oddest thing happened (as if nothing odd had happened already). Mod stopped shouting. There was a sudden stillness in the landscape. The wind was no longer moving the trees, and the sound of the waterfall retreated into the distance. A flat, fist-sized piece of mica, larger than the ones that had rained down on my head, floated down from the sky and landed in front of me.

Mod looked at me and said, *"Pick it up. It's all right now."*

"What's all right now, Mod?" I asked. *"What's all right?"*

"The leprechauns don't like humans getting too close to them. Everything around here can feel you. They don't normally register humans. But they can feel you. They were trying to scare you away." She paused a minute in her monologue.

Then she continued. *"I just told them what happened by the monastery. I told them that the ghosts wouldn't haunt that area anymore. They can go back to that part of their land now. I told them that the faery sang for you. They are sorry. The leprechauns aren't often sorry. So they sent you a gift."*

I had that gift of mica for many years. I carried it on the plane with me whenever I came to Ireland. Every time I walked the path to the top of the waterfall in Glendalough, I would stop, sit on the rock, and thank the leprechauns for accepting me. I didn't take that acceptance lightly.

"Fair Sligo thee I now must leave,
To part thy beauty I do grieve,
But not forever, I believe, I'll call again to Sligo."

—*Lyrics & Music by Carmel Gunning*

chapter seven

Meeting Brendan

The first time that Brendan came for a reading, I was surprised. I could sense that he kept to himself far away in a rural part of Ireland and was not drawn to come into the bustling, frantic city of Dublin. But here he was. His body was lanky and yet muscles rippled beneath his simple white shirt. I had the feeling that he wore some version of that ensemble every day--simple pants and shirt, with a traditional Irish vest.

He was very quiet when he sat down and yet there was an air about him that put me off. It could have been that he thought he was better than anyone else, but something in me did not think that was the entire story. He actually unnerved me and it felt good to retreat into the space within which the mystical engagement of a consultation occurs. As I moved deeper and deeper into his psyche and the mystery of his being, a wondrous stream of experience began to occur. More wondrous than most.

The experience of being with Brendan during his consult took me back into my childhood where fantasy and 'reality' seemed to be pretty much one and the same thing. I was in wonderland with him. A strange other worldly portal beckoned.

I truly love doing consults. They are magical, whether they are a bumpy ride or a smooth one. I relax and enjoy the template of existence I am privileged to when I read. I have learned that no matter how unusual it feels as I open up my mind to the other and see what there was to see, the person I am working with is startled by the relevance of what I was saying.

I do not need to believe or disbelieve what I am saying. I just need to be present to what there was to say. When I am working in person, the body language of the person often changes. In the beginning there is often a 'frozen in place' type of body language or twitching or squirming.

For clients, having someone they have never met, in this case me, delve into the depth of who they are and who they came here to be can be a bit unnerving. Yet as they feel known and seen for who they truly are, they relax. As their destiny is revealed and the problems they are experiencing begin to make sense, a relief and a calm occur.

When the barriers to consciousness open and the flow of the true self is present, the veil of denial that shrouds the majesty of who people really are gives way. The connection to that truth is sublime and I feel the grace of it in my soul.

With Brendan, the more present I became, the more I wanted to believe what I saw--a world that was as clear as the world I lived in every day. Except that this world carried deep connections to the inner Earth and Her elemental beings.

I looked over at Brendan and he was glowing, a strange transparent glowing. He was looking past me, not at something, but in the presence of something that gave him life, not a memory, a world.

That world was paintable. A glowing cloud of transparent energy surrounded the regal, elfin young man. A single tear rolled down his cheek, perfectly timed with the stillness of the energy and his gaze. I almost stopped speaking, but then realized that I mustn't bring him out of what was moving in him. Breathing and moving into what was calling to be revealed, I discovered that a single tear was rolling down my cheek too.

I don't remember much about the reading after that, except that he said, *"When are you coming to Sligo to stay with me?"* It was not an invitation. It was a command given by an emissary from a mysterious realm. A command that I had learned to obey.

Three Weeks Later

Brendan picked me up at the bus station. He was the caretaker of an estate on Glencar Lake in Sligo, an old hunting lodge that he looked after for the owners, who used it as a vacation home. The lake was well known in an unusual way. A book *Pi in the Sky* spoke of a powerful vortex there. That vortex was right in front of the boathouse on the property. I didn't know that at the time. I suppose people think that someone who works in what is commonly called a 'psychic medium' would have a more active knowledge of where vortexes are, what vortexes are, and what is important about them.

Frankly, I have always been busy being so engaged in multidimensional realities and coping with experiencing them, that I never felt the need to understand them. I am designed to sit in the awe and wonder of the sunset rather than describe and understand its properties. However during this visit, I would have appreciated a little bit more understanding in this area.

In books people say, *"Well, one thing led to the next!"* I never quite realized how potent that statement could be. So let me say here, *"You wouldn't believe how one thing led to the next and the next and the next."* Each thing was completely powerful and stunning in its own right. Another phrase that is often used is, *"just when I thought it was over...."* Between 'one thing led to the next' and 'just when I thought it was over' is one whopper of a tale.

It all started innocently enough. We went to his caretaker house and he took my overnight bag in. The house was small and made of wood, clean beyond the norm, as if dust and dirt were repelled in some way. I remember realizing that he had built some of the furniture and it looked like he had polished the walls. Also there in the ordinary was the glow of the not ordinary. The same glow I had seen in the consult. Ah, but that is the way of the magic.

Perhaps if you went there, you would see nothing that I saw. Perhaps if I went back there it would not be the same for me.

But that day, I remember being struck by how much someone could accomplish if they never had anything to do with human beings. His antisocial briskness and his unbridled cantankerousness made it very clear he had me there for some other reason than his love of humanity. I think being in that kind of discomfort befuddled my memory, but even in the discomfort, something was present that I had never experienced before--in the floorboards, the walls, the furniture--even in the air. While I was busy attempting to adjust to this surreal environment, he took me outside to his chickens.

Yes, he took me to see his chickens, every kind of chicken you could ever imagine. He had imported them from all over the world. Some of them were so attractive I couldn't take my eyes off of them. Some of them looked so weird I couldn't take my eyes off of them. Tall tufted white plumes on one chicken's head made it look like it was always on the verge of falling over. Another chicken had such iridescent metallic colors, I wondered if it was a live chicken or a statue. The potpourri of colors and strutting and cackling moved without pause through thirty or forty chickens.

These chickens, some looking like caricatures from Mardi Gras, were surrounded by half that number of equally unusual looking roosters promenading in the enclosure especially made for them. Some of the full-grown roosters were so small, they would fit into your palm and others were the size of a small turkey.

When Brendan came near however, they swiftly gathered around him. I couldn't get over what was happening. This bevy of chickens and roosters were related to him. He and they were a family. I found myself dizzy from the strangeness of his attitude, the house that had special unexplainable properties and now, not a chicken coop, but a sanctuary for a community of fowls and a human.

I felt like I was a visitor from another planet and they were the real planetary residents.

He watched me attentively. I was clearly being examined to see if I qualified. For what I didn't know. I prayed that it was nothing sinister. I thought to myself, *"Idiot! No one knows where you are! You don't even know where you are! You don't even know this person really!"*

Ask anyone worth their salt who does psychic work, how often we can read the soul of someone and they are not yet in their actual life what we read. People would always, at some time in the future, become what I saw, but I didn't know if I might be fatefully off in this case. However, the persistent beckoning that had pursued me since I came to Ireland had drawn me here and I knew I had become its ally and its friend.

I looked over at him and realized that I had already surrendered to the mystery. I felt him relax and actually smile. He got very quiet and reflective and I knew we were moving into the next phase of 'next' and 'just when I thought'. I relaxed, went into a space of connection, and let energy surround me and enfold me just in case I might be in any danger. The next minute I felt like I had been touched, but it was all right. I had reached that state where whatever was to transpire, I could completely open to it.

I came forward into my mind, located him with my senses, opened my eyes and saw that he too had entered a state of oneness with what was to be.

"So at the end of this day, we give thanks
For being betrothed to the unknown."

—*John O'Donohue*

chapter eight

A Room Built for Me

Later that evening, Brendan told me he wanted to take me somewhere. I have to admit that fear was chattering away, but I had consciously chosen surrender, no matter what might occur.

We walked down the road from his home onto a trail that led into a fertile woodland of trees and gigantic rhododendrons. I looked up and all around me were green encircling mountains. Brendan explained to me that in those mountains the legend of Queen Maeve was born. Maeve was the goddess of Connaught, the most rural region of southern Ireland. When Christianity arrived in the area, the monks were intrigued by the local tales and couldn't help but tell them. Not wanting to acknowledge the gods and goddesses, they referred to them as kings, queens, chieftains, and the like. Maeve was so powerful a legend for the people they soon worked to ridicule her but even in those tales her essence shined through. As legend had it, the kings claimed kingship only through her. She was referred to as having many husbands and she used to offer men the friendship of her thighs!! No wonder the monks loved her so much. Maeve's legendary cairn, the Gaelic word for tomb, was directly opposite us on top of Knocknarea Mountain.

Brendan, I was sure, was her emissary.

The road was lined with giant rhododendron. In America, rhododendrons are trees found in the mountains and in the suburbs, large but not overwhelming. Here they towered way over our heads and blocked out the light. Their gnarled limbs wound so tightly together, they overtook everything in their path. I saw he had cut a pathway through them about four people wide. I asked him how he did that. He said dismissively, *"With a chainsaw."*

It was breathtaking.

I realized, as I walked with him, that he had prepared this white, pink and rose garlanded avenue for me and had been doing this since the day I had said I would come. *"Why?!"* I thought. Then I remembered his tears that day during the consult. I realized no one had ever gotten inside the magical reality of his existence before. And I, as a seer, had gotten in and been touched by being there.

He had felt my longing and recognized that it was his long-ing too. The magic restores the longings of magical children who have been taken from their native lands and thrown into the lands of banal flavorless mediocrity. Magical lands find their way to their lost children. Finding another who moves with enchantment is rare indeed. But to find another who can mutually share it, that is what Brendan had hoped when he invited me.

Sensing this, I organized myself to be as equally present to the wellspring of enchantment as he was. I did not know if I would succeed. Maybe I had been around too many 'normal' people for too long. The realm of 'the magic' was always near me but had always honored my staying in the 'normal' world.

I had always hoped that someday I could build a bridge be-tween the everyday rat race of civilization and the realm of the wild magic. That dream felt far away--that dream to see unicorns run down the streets of New York City--and other such 'fantasies'. But here I was with a young man who was either absolutely mad, yet beautifully mysterious in his mad-ness, or a two legged creature who had truly become one with the wild magic.

What is the wild magic? The wild magic is all around us. Mostly we see it in nature in weather--rainbows, hailstorms, flashfloods and fires. It has no interest in giving in to hu-mans. Some of us know the realm of the wild magic. The wild magic lives in the soft brown eyes of a sika deer stand-ing in the gold straw grass of the Glendalough mountains watching you, unmoving, including you, ears twitching, opening up portals around you so subtlety that you don't realize it until you have come down from the mountain and it is many more hours later than it should be.

The wild magic tickles your feet when you find you MUST reach a large stone sticking up in the middle of a bubbling creek in the middle of nowhere in the heartlands. Climbing over twigs, sliding on the moist ferns, gingerly attempting to balance on the slippery water rocks, finally reaching the stone, feeling chagrin from your foolishness, your hiking boots soaked from losing your footing, you sit down and begin to cry.

Tears burst the seams of your heart as you feel the water include you, touching you with a charm that soaks your isolated soul with lost memories of belonging. Those are the sweetest moments a life can have. Sometimes the wild magic trains you to be respectful, restoring your reverence for life in very unpleasant ways. Ah, but that is in another part of the tale.

As the afternoon light began to fade, I wished that I had on a long flowing white gown and that my hair was plaited with flowers winding their way between hair and air. I let myself feel the dress that wasn't there. I pretended I had bare feet that felt the moist inviting soil and the silent music that guided my every step. Surrendering, surrendering... surrendering. I yielded into the energy of his presence and the wonder of a place that was formed out of the crafts of his hands.

Craftsmanship and art were the bridges of the past where magic and man met, now no more--except maybe here.

We rounded a corner. There in the center of this tangled massive forest of mountain laurel and trees, he had carved out a room. Everything caught my eyes at once. In front of me in the center of the room was a table. The table was tilted. The one side leaning toward the ground, I realized, fit me. I was the one who sat in the three-foot seat. His seat was in front of the table that pointed at an angle toward the trees. His seat was made for a five-foot ten-inch long legged elf.

The tilt was only part of the charm of the table. The other charming features were in the large grail designed cups carved with bases that slanted to fit the table and the thin slices of tree trunks that served as plates, rough on the bottom so that they didn't slide off into our laps.

While I was busy staring wide-eyed at the mastery of the ingenious craftsmanship, he disappeared down the trail. The end of the day burst alive with light, coming closer and closer, until I could see that he was lighting lanterns made from the twisted vines of the laurel. Each unique lantern held one single candle lit with a flame that did not flicker.

As he came toward me up the lane, I knew that I had officially left the world of the ordinary.

"Time out of mind
Must be heavenly
It's all enchanted and wild
It's just like my heart said
It was going to be"

'Out of the Woods'
—Sinead Lohan

CHAPTER NINE

The Beings

I had never met someone who embodied the silence as powerfully as Brendan. As he came back into the open space where we were to dine, his silence permeated the forest. Everything was still. This was quite a contrast to the background noise that had been there when we first came into the grove. Then the stream that flowed against the rhododendron mega-bushes had been a babbling gurgle. Now the stream shared the silence.

The silence was palpable, as if something was present and yet not in the same dimension I was in. I could see the tree-like bushes of the flowering rhododendron moving with the mountain breeze, slightly twisting and turning the branches. This was not the straight flow of the wind coming through the valley. The wind coming through the branches flowed in silence.

Suddenly, I was spent. From the work I had done with people through the years, including the eons before I returned to this planet, I knew that when an experience was so outside the realm of possibility for a human being, an instant kind of narcolepsy can happen. Sudden fatigue, an almost blacking out of the senses would occur. I was aware that this was happening and I also knew that I could not fight it.

Brendan, completely in sync with my need to suddenly lie down, was pulling back the multi-level bedding on the stuffed mattress held by closely woven vines. These vines nestled in a sea of many-petaled soft white flowers with bold, broad, rigid leaves.

Rhododendrons come either as bushes or trees. These were both. Tall treed boughs of flowers, sparkling with the last light of the sun, towered over me. Around me, the close bunched branches of flowers encircled my giant mattress, which was stuffed with cloth and feathers, then covered with soft cotton and wool blankets.

Brendan held back the covers and helped me crawl into the hammock-like bed. I obeyed dutifully, even though I was concerned that I would sink down so completely into the bushes that he would have to cut me out. But no, the bed not only held, it moved up and down when I shifted my weight. The bushes seemed to move to accommodate my body, like lying with a lover and the shifting that occurs to maximize the embrace.

My back was to Brendan, so I did not see him leave, but I felt him leave. I was so amazed at how safe I felt. It was uncanny, the sense of being part of the trees, the bushes, the flowers, the streams. I didn't mind that I was engulfed in silence. The silence felt original, like I was part of some original world of inherent belonging. A pang of sadness gripped me for a moment because I could feel how my life felt without that completeness and I longed to live in this space of nothing missing, an 'everything' present.

A simple melody played on a reed flute floated up out of the silence. The sound captured the rustle of the wind moving through the trees. The melody wove a spell through the strange shaped table, the vined bench, my nature canopy bed, moving, touching, including, until the webbing of enchanting inclusive music touched the stream. Dainty twinkling tones escalated into a swirling orchestration of multitones coming from everywhere, until the energy and sound encased me in a vortex that was my room, my place in the universe that celebrated my being there. I slept.

I woke up the next morning to find Brendan standing there in his more normal mode of one foot impatiently patting the ground, arms folded, clearly waiting on me to rise. Again he helped me from my cocoon, and we sat down to eat the delicious fresh eggs from his chickens. He was very agitated and shifted sideways, then toward me, clearly wanting to say something and not knowing what to say.

Finally he blurted out, *"I need to take you somewhere."*

In that one statement, I was clear that somehow the night before, what he had expected had not occurred. I realized that, with his less than optimistic opinion of human beings, he had set up the evening to reveal some lack of sensitivity on my part and my being so sensitive and accepting had somehow really upset him. I realized that like all human beings, Brendan had gotten used to his dreams not coming true, and at this moment in his life, a woman from the USA was resonant with what he was showing her.

He had taken a gamble inviting me. He had been asked by the primordial forces that he had an intimate relationship with, to bring me here and now to take me somewhere. I was clear he never thought it would get this far. Having our dreams and visions come true can be an upsetting thing. We have learned to be who we are without them.

More than that, I realized that he had been charged with being a messenger and he was not particularly fond of that idea.

I said, *"Okay."*

I stood up and left the table, making sure to balance the goblet that I'd drained of orange juice so that it did not fall to the ground. Everything suddenly felt precarious and I didn't want to make any foolish unconscious mistakes. Without a word, Brendan turned away from the table and walked straight into the woods. I quickly followed.

I hadn't realized there was another gap in the rhododendron forest. Until you walked toward it, you could not see it, a thin opening with just enough room to maneuver through the branches. I followed Brendan. I did not miss the way the branches moved just enough to grant him passage. I also did not miss they were not so forthcoming with me.

A bit disheveled, I stepped out into a shaded meadow. The rhododendron had changed into weathered old trees that lined an open meadow, yet at the same time leaned in and shaded it. A thick tree had fallen on the far side, blocking an open area beyond.

Brendan pointed to the downed tree and said, *"Crawl over it and go into the next meadow."*

I did not even say 'yah' or 'nay'. I just began walking. The congeniality of the night before gone, I dared not disobey this time.

Crawling over the downed tree was daunting. It was far thicker than I realized, so I had to lie across it, swing one leg over it and then use gravity to slide the rest of me over to the ground beyond. I stood up, brushed off the tree bark and turned to walk on.

Somehow when I crossed over the tree, I had crossed over into another dimension. What I had seen from where I had been standing with Brendan had vanished.

I stood in a shivering field of energy and in front of me forty-foot-high Beings looked down at me. My mind buckled.

In what was just seconds but felt like an eternity, my mind searched for a sensible explanation for what the optic nerve was sending into its brain.

"These are trees," spit out of my desperate mind.

"But they are not trees," my knowing said.

I screamed, "No!!!!!!!!" as my carefully constructed mental concepts of reality sought to overwhelm what I was clearly present to.

I screamed again, "NOOOOOOOOOOO!!!" stopping the thoughts in their tracks so that the wonder of what was in front of me would not recede.

The beings looked down on me, patiently waiting to see what would occur.

I felt the fringes of insanity give way to knowing, for when I screamed, "NOOOO!!" for the last time, a strong burst of energy threw me up into the air and landed me about five feet from where I had been standing.

Boy, if you ever wanted evidence that we are made of energy, when my mind opened up and let go and the door blew open into another dimension of reality, the power of that created an energetic explosion that knocked me just like a raw electrical circuit knocks you across the floor when it is not grounded.

I crawled back to the downed tree and sat leaning back against it, looking up at the giant slim effervescent beings that were looking down at me.

There was no transmission. I didn't go away with anything other than that I had made contact with something that was there, that in our entrapped minds we never know is there being with us, being part of a bigger reality, being part of our existence.

I fell asleep eventually, so grateful that my mind had blown open. I knew now there would be so much more to see. The closed in walls of mind that had happened to me when I was young, had burst free. I had no idea how life would be, but

I knew that I had my mind back. I don't know how human beings exist in such a closed in state of mind. I had known for years that I could not, and now I didn't have to.

When I awoke, Brendan was sitting beside me crying. I started crying too. My big ole body curled up in the arms of the tall spindly young'un. We shared space, a space most human beings never get to share with the world of wonder that surrounds us.

We walked back to his cottage. I sat outside while he fixed a late lunch. I watched his chickens that he had gathered from all over the world. I was enveloped in the love of being human. *"This is why we came,"* I realized. We came to blend in with the marvels of this earth and to experience the richness of the multi-dimensional realms all around us that love us and adore us.

I thought, *"What on earth have we been doing?"*

"Will you lay all of your deepest wildest secrets bare?
Will you let all of those rumbling old gods take rage?
I want to be there when the savage comes!
I want to be there when the savage comes--
when your savage earth heart cuts through!"

'Savage Earth Heart'
—Sinead O'Connor

chapter ten

The Piper Stones

I returned to Ireland a year later. I found another B&B, leaving Mrs. Brady to her Bushmills. Mod had faded back into her world. Brendan returned to his chickens. I still worked at the centre in Dublin.

Those first years I would meet people who became my guides and my messengers. They introduced me to areas of Ireland I had not seen. They would come for a while and then they would be gone...back into their modern lives in their modern worlds. I can never thank these people enough for their role in my unfolding during those years. These are but a few of the stories I could tell.

Naomi was one of those guides. This day, we were on our way to the Piper stones. Naomi, my driver, a British client, deftly dodged oncoming cars, most of them headed straight at us as we rounded corners. There were no white lines down the center of the road, and no shoulders, either.

Years later, after they put in a major superhighway across the small county, I jokingly said to my friend Richard, *"I don't get it. Even with lines on the road, the Irish still drive where they want and completely ignore the lines."* He looked at me and smiled, *"Don't you know? They put the lines in for you Americans. You always try to stay between the lines."* Once again I was slagged, one of Ireland's own putting an uppity 'foreigner' in her place.

We got out of the car, and I thought, *"What on earth is significant about these? And why had we driven two and a half hours, on winding, single lane roads that masqueraded as a two-lane highway, to see them?"*

As we climbed up to the stones, my feet mired down with each step. I struggled to cross the web-rooted tapestry of bog, where one step with just a little too much pressure, had you up to your privates in mud. When we finally arrived on solid ground, I stared at yet another non-tourist site circle of stones. The first stones I came to were spaced about ten feet apart. They were gray, hammered into square-shaped stones, about three by three. Usually, at most of the circles, there was an unexplainable silence, even for the circle that was right in the middle of the large town of Killarney. The silence here felt disturbed in some way, an unmistakable beckoning.

"Well, I'm not about to be beckoned today," I thought. *"I have been beckoned enough, by gosh by golly!"* I decided I would politely walk the circled stones that spread a distance across the sunny landscape for my client's sake. She was so excited about bringing me out here. I shallowly thanked the stones for being there, as was my normal ritual, this time not heart-felt, and began to walk the circle.

Everything seemed fine until I walked past a spread-out dark green tree that appeared to have no trunk. Or if it was there, the trunk consisted of thick limbs that crawled everywhere across the ground. The foliage, dark, flat elephant ear leaves, which were disproportionate to the size of the thin deflated limbs of the tree, jutted out, as if seeking escape.

That now-common skin crawling, spine-terrifying feeling began again. I thought, "Enough already!" Stoically making my way around the limbs of the grounded tree, I didn't notice what was in front of me. When I looked up, the ten-foot spaced, three-foot squared standing stones were gone! In their place was a row of rounded white stones. White half globes about four feet wide looked as if they had simply, or maybe not so simply, popped out of the ground. They were exquisite! While they were rough to the touch, there was a crystal sheen that made them iridescent.

Naomi was standing there waiting on me. Again, the cumulative fatigue of the constant barrage of the new and unknown enveloped me. All I could say was, *"I am so sorry. I have to lie down and rest."*

My British client was clearly offended that I was not marveling at the discovery. She was large, like me, high waisted and a bit proper. It hadn't been that easy for her to trek out to the stones, either. As she disappeared behind the curious tree, she said, *"Look out for the pipers. These are the Piper Stones, you know. Legend has it that pipers were making music during a festival and dancing in a circle on a Holy Day. Such activity was strictly forbidden and the anger of the gods at this blasphemous behavior was so great that they turned the pipers into stones."*

I didn't care. I stretched out on one of the rounded stones, curling into a fetal position so I could stay balanced on the dome of the stone. The stones lined a three to four foot high embankment. I fell asleep wondering why they were put there. Decoration? Probably not. Communication? Maybe. The thoughts ran though my mind as I drifted into sleep.

"Top of the day to you, my lady!" I jerked awake. *"Quite the morning, isn't it?"*

Still curled up, I looked around, but there was no one in sight. I struggled to roll over and still saw nothing, as the persistent male voice spoke again.

"Y' here to see where the last Druids were buried?"

"Where are you?" I replied, praying someone was actually there.

"I'm right here," he replied, which in Irish is completely accurate and yet gets you no further than where you were before, and often even more confused.

"Where is here?" I shouted, glad at least that the voice was somewhere.

Rolling over on my belly, I looked behind the stone, which overlooked the embankment. I came face-to-face and eye-to-eye with the shortest man I had ever seen. We were practically nose-to-nose, as he tipped his rumpled Irish tweed cap.

"Well, do you want to see the graves or not?"

"Could I be seeing a real leprechaun?" I thought, *"Or at least a leprechaun's ancestor?"*

"Tom's the name" he went on. *"I got waked up this morn to come get the lady asleep on the Piper Stones."* He was beaming with his mission accomplished.

"Yes, of course I want to see them," I replied, having absolutely no idea what made me say that.

"Well, let's go then. The other lady's in the car waiting for us."

As I worked my way to a standing posture and walked toward the edge of the bog, the Irish cap was all I could see on the other side of the stones. Then, a perfectly wrinkled face, right out of a storybook drawing of an elder leprechaun, appeared. His sun-baked face let me know he had dug a lot of peat out of the bog lands.

His body appeared as he walked up the slope, level with me. He wore a Sunday brown woolen coat over a high-necked dark brown Sunday shirt, baggy brown pants, and Sunday shoes without a spot of bog on them. I am 5'5" tall. All I could think was, "He is so short!" He came up to my elbow.

Tom guided me along a path that led to the cars. Much easier than the "slog the bog" way I came. Tom was parked behind us. His car was well used and packed with children of all ages.

"This's the missus, herself," he said proudly, as he pointed out

the lovely, weathered, small-boned woman holding a robust baby in the front seat.

"I found the lady!" he beamed to his wife, to the car, and to the surrounding landscape.

"Follow me," he said.

I scrambled to get into the car with Naomi as his small overloaded car shot out in front of us. *"Forget the seat belt!"* I shouted. *"Let's go!"*

All fatigue was gone. I knew two things – I did not want to get lost in the back roads of Ireland, and now I wanted desperately, for some unknown reason, to see the last of the Druid graves.

What a journey. Right! Then suddenly left! Then left, then left again. It was clear Naomi knew how to follow an Irishman. Tom's car stopped suddenly at a gate that opened into farmed land. I could see a small knoll in the middle of the tilled ground that was crowded with tall, shapely trees.

Tom appeared at my side of the car, opened the door, and said to Naomi, *"You need to stay with the car. This is for the lady."* Not waiting to see or hear her response, I leapt out of the car, and Tom and I headed for the gate alone.

St. Patrick, at one time, burnt one hundred and eighty books of the Druids. "Such an example," he said, "set the converted Christians to work in all parts, until, in the end, all the remains of the Druidic superstition were utterly destroyed."

—The author of 'The Lecan',
an ancient Irish manuscript

CHAPTER ELEVEN

The Knoll

Tom held the gate open for me and I passed through. I was listening to the sounds of the children in the car and watching the flurry of the birds swooping up, down, and across the golden ground prepared for planting. Then I felt it. The air got sharper. Tom went on ahead toward the knoll but I held still.

After many years of feeling when a state shift in reality is beginning to occur, I know when to stop and observe. I know when to listen, and when to open myself up into what I am in touch with and/or what is contacting me. I feel different physically.

This day as I held still, I felt softer, more rural. I felt a long skirt wafting against my legs from the minuscule wind that whispered across the ground. I felt a simple blouse and a home-woven shawl, coarse and warm around my shoulders. These experiences let me know I was entering into another dimension, in this case, another time.

I looked over the fence at the car loaded with Tom's children. Two of the boys, probably between eight and ten years old, were shoving each other. The older girl in her mid teens was pushing them away from her as she was pinned between them and the two younger children on the other side of her. A young girl around five, curly headed with erratically distributed hair, was bending over the front seat playing with the newest addition to the family. The last child, with chopped black bowl-cut hair, was indistinguishable as male or female. His or her face was plastered against the window that didn't roll all the way down. A small round three-year-old face with owl-like black eyes was staring, not at me but at the knoll straight ahead.

I turned to follow the child's gaze. It looked as if wavy hot air was rising from the ground, masking the knoll in an eerie spectrum, like the mirages you see in the desert. Everything looked wobbly behind the wall of air, undulating against the knoll.

Urgency rose again, and I hurried toward the knoll, clearly feeling my legs caught in my non-existent skirt, clipping along in my heavy work boots passed down to me by a 'not this lifetime' brother.

Before I reached the knoll something caught my eye, off to my left. I turned toward it and started running toward the hills on the other side of the road.

"No! No! No!" I screamed. My present day weight was no longer a hindrance. My past life memory took over my heart and my soul. I could see it all... wagons racing across the tree-cleared land. Some of them were colorful, like gypsy wagons all decked out with tassels and bells, brightly painted in a myriad of rainbow colors. The round-shaped wagons were driven by men. You could see the women and children hanging on as the wagons lunged for the surrounding hillsides. Men in long robes tied with coarse rope belts, their heads hooded and carrying staffs sped along beside the wagons on foot.

"Noooo! Look out!!!" I cried, falling to my knees, not wanting to see but unable to cover my eyes. The soldiers came straight at them from the very hills the wagons were racing toward seeking safety. I felt the phantom soldiers on horseback brush against me as they closed in on them.

Sabers drawn. Slash! Slash! Slash! The sabers cut through the harnesses, killing the horses to stop the wagons. The robed men shied away from the wagons, knowing they were the goal, clearly hoping the soldiers would follow them. Even that did not stop the slaughter.

The cruel queen of England, who imprisoned the Irish queens and kings, had calculated what was now needed to break the back of this strong, spirited land. Kill the Druids.

Some of the soldiers turned and headed toward the Druids. The hooded men, the people's Druids, stood in a circle, back to back, their hoods thrown back. White-bearded old men stood with clean-shaven younger men. They lifted their staffs to the skies.

The wind roared awake all around them. The soldiers' horses bolted, throwing the soldiers to the ground. Nervous, the soldiers at the wagons stopped the carnage. The screams of the dying women and children subsided. The world paused.

Then the fury of the Queen's soldiers, the barren, lonely Queen spilling the blood of an ancient land for the sake of conquest alone, turned on the gathered Druids. How dare these hooded men hold authority over their Queen? How dare the love of these lower-than-dogs peasants for these barefooted, ragged men be greater than their love for their Queen? Enraged, they drove their horses into the center of the Druids.

Sobbing, screaming, I now begged the hearts of these merciless men to not murder the last of our wise men, our Druids.

I rushed toward them. Caught in the middle of the phantom scene, I held on to the oldest Druid, trying to shield him with my body. He smiled at me as the saber cut through his head. I fell with him, tears flooding the blood that pulsed out of him. The phantom bodies of the last Druids fell all around me.

There was no Christian prayer coming from the wounded and dying Celts. Prayer was only for the one-god worshippers who had brought the treachery of a Lord and Savior to their land.

There was only the cry, the scream, the wail, the rocking back and forth... calling on the soul of The Mother, crying the names of the gods and goddesses of their sacred ways, to take their souls back to where life continued unencumbered by the horror of the interlopers, the plague of their land.

I heard them before I saw them, angry-eyed, blood-raged, running from everywhere, running for the soldiers.

"AAAAAAAAAAAAeeeeeeeeeeeeeeeeeee!

AAAAAAAAAAAAAAAAAAhhhhhhhhhhh

Yahhhhhhhhhhhhhhhhhhhhhh!

HAEEEEEEEEEeeeeeeeee!"

Their fierce, throbbing, guttural sounds pierced the sky as their run-ning feet pounded the ground. The hair on my neck stood up as the power of their wild chanting coursed through my blood, the blood of my people.

I watched as the villagers, merchants, farmers, mothers, and children clubbed the heads of the soldiers' horses until they dropped dead to the ground. They stabbed the soldiers with pitchforks. The stronger men whacked the torsos of the soldiers with axes, while the smaller women and children jumped on the downed soldiers, stabbing them with knives long after they died.

Women ran for the dying and wounded, holding them, keening the sounds of death into the air. The soldiers fled in all directions to no avail. They had done the abominable. They were to die abominably.

Some of the women and men reached the Druids and me. The ghosts of another time wrapped each body carefully and quickly, covering each one with holly berries, oak leaves, and their own blood as they spilled open their palms, linking their blood with the blood of their dead Druids.

With the wagon horses dead, they harnessed themselves to the wag-ons and began to move forward toward a high knoll in the center of a small forest. I watched the ghost men and women hauling those wagons with their precious loads as they faded into a time long gone.

Now alone on the modern landscape of now, Tom held me in his arms, rocking me back and forth with his small but sturdy body. Collapsed into his arms, I wept.

"Oh, my lady," Tom cried, *"Oh, my lady."* Again the wordless understanding of the Celtic heart would warm my bleeding soul. *"Come on my lady, let's get up now. Let's go see them now."*

As I stood, I realized how far I had come from the knoll. The now solitary knoll was no longer surrounded by the small forest of the past. Only a few trees remained.

"They never found them, my lady. They searched and searched, spilled our blood, maimed us, burned us out, but we never told. We spelled the knoll, my lady, with blood. The soldiers always veered away when they came near, never realizing something was changing their course. Many years later, after the murder of our Druids was forgotten, we put up ogham stones to honor them."

We reached the knoll. Until you stepped up into the carpet of pine needles and oak leaves, you only saw trees. Until you stepped up off the farmed land, you saw nothing else. Stepping onto the treed knoll, I could see, cupped in the hollows of downed trees, the stones. Dark, mottled-with-age stones cut like large three-foot fingers with markings. Slashes and lines through the slashes marked the ancient Celtic ogham alphabet of being.

I went straight to the tallest stone away from the rest, standing free. I knew this was the grave of the high Druid. I don't know how long I sat there hugging the stone, sobbing gut wrenching sobs for a world now gone, yet so longed for.

The sun was making its way toward the horizon when I finally looked up and saw Tom standing guard, his hands clasped behind his back. An ode to a powerful reverence surrounded him. I felt the wind. I stood up. I held up my arms to the sky.

The wind responded, gathering strength. Currents of air laced their fingers through the trees, twirling them, swinging their strong limbs this way and that. I opened up my arms wide and laughed. Faster and faster the breeze spun the pine and oak leaves into whirling dervishes of nature, spinning like tops as they flew off the trees onto the ground.

As the wind released them, the trees bowed, and then raised their limbs high toward the heavens. They would have danced if their roots would have let them. Joy coursed through me. Tom shouted over the cacophony of the shrill of wood to wood and the clap of leaf to leaf. He shouted his elation, words dancing across the field to his wife who was standing with their children at the gate bordering the field, "She's got the ways, missus! She's got the ways!"

I knew who I was now. I was a Druid alive with the magic. I laughed as I cried, filled and overflowing from the breathtaking, life-giving bliss of the ancient ways. I raised my hands and called the ravens in the ancient signing of the ancient goddesses of this ancient land. They came. The sky darkened with the black birds coming from all directions, drowning the sound of the wind with their cries. They filled the trees, creating a dark-spotted landscape as the sun left the sky.

"She's got the touch, missus!" Tom cried.

I fell to my knees and opened up my arms, no longer a tourist, but an ancient Druidess, with the ways of nature at her call. I embraced my beloved leprechaun. We curled up together, sitting with our backs against the tallest stone watching the ravens return to the ordinary world in the night sky. We held hands, listening to the ancient silence that surrounded the knoll.

Finally one of Tom's boys came up to us. Shaking his father's shoulder, he whispered, *"Mum says ya gotta come, Da. It's supper time."*

" Night owns my white bones but
What's left is still saying
Strange prayers in high places
Wild airs with wilder graces
Birds fly with no motion
What draws me draws the ocean "

'Still Believing'
—Mary Black

chapter twelve

Fungi

One day, at the end of a consult, a young woman, arms bangled and tattooed and dressed in a long cotton skirt topped by a body-revealing tank top invited me to join her friend and herself on a trip to Cork that evening to hear Richard Waterborn, a gifted teacher and healer. Drawn to go, I said yes.

Arriving in Cork, the talk had already begun. We snuck into the back of a well packed living room while Richard was speaking.

"There is in every one of us a place where we remember everything of

*any significance which has ever happened to us. This 'cellular mem-
ory' is part of our biology, something we share with the simplest of
life-forms. Whilst our every day rational mind filters out any disturbing memory or emotionally overwhelming experience in order to get on
with the tasks of life, our cellular memory records everything--right
back to the very beginning of our life up to the present day. Indeed,
some of these memories may extend beyond this lifetime- -to the womb
or even beyond, to what may be other life experiences.....”*

As a cellular empath, I was aware, in a way that few people
recognized, much less could converse about. That evening
was a turning point in my own recognition of what was
maturing in me. Finally here was someone to talk with
who grasped what it might be like to be a cellular empath.
I was invited to stay the night so we could talk. The girls
said they would take me back the next morning to Dublin.
"Cork is a great party town!" The tattooed beauty called back
as they left the house.

Richard and I stayed up until morning, modern day alche-
mists sharing what we had discovered, both in our healing
work and in our exploration of what was happening in the
cellular memories of human beings during these times. The
only sleep I got was the three-hour ride back to the Spiritual
Centre. It didn't matter. I was alive with the joy of being
with someone who was aware of my kind of experiences.

Richard invited me to come to Cork to work at his home the
next time I came. Part of his house was his healing centre.
I had to smile. I would be working on the top floor, which
was exactly the same number of floors up as the Dublin
centre...only the steps were wider!

Richard and I became fast friends. He was a witness to not only my journey in Ireland, but also my unfolding into who I was becoming for the future.

Once we were sitting out in his car. It was raining so hard, we couldn't see out. He was theorizing about what was happening to the consciousness of human beings. I was so agitated. Everything he was talking about was happening to me. Finally I shoved him and said, *"I am not theory! I am right here!"*

We both, in that moment, remembered, what we knew applied to real people with real lives, including ourselves.

Six months later, I flew into Shannon Airport. Mary, Richard's slim, pretty partner, picked me up. She reared Richard's kids, worked as a therapist, and managed the very active household. She was a soul sister. I fell in love with her. We hardworking women shared about our lives on our drive to Cork.

I worked in Cork for two weeks; then Richard and I took our first of many road trips. I was facilitating my first residential workshop on Inis Mor (Árainn na Naomh), the largest of the Aran Islands on the Atlantic side of Ireland, the coming weekend.

Richard wanted to take me to Dingle to meet a famous mammal who swam in Dingle Bay. Fungi had been named by a woman who swam with him after her husband died. After she swam with Fungi, in her wetsuit in the dark deep waters of Dingle Bay, she remembered her husband without any sense of loss or grief. Whatever had separated them in death separated them no more. However, who knows what possessed her to call a dolphin the size of a small orca whale 'Fungi'.

Dingle was three hours away. We would get to Dingle early, spend time with Fungi, and stay the night. That gave us plenty of time for the five hour drive to the Ros a' Mhils Ferry to the Aran Islands the next day. Driving anywhere in Ireland was worth the jaunt providing hours of great conversation and startling views.

I had been coming to Ireland for over two years now. I was familiar with 'Irish time'. Never how long it takes, only how important it is to go.

There are those of the magic and Richard was one of them. When he felt strongly about something, I knew to go along.

Richard said we would drive to where Fungi was usually spotted, near the shore of the bay. I was amazed as Richard described this now famous dolphin of Dingle Bay. Fungi had been in Dingle Bay over thirty years, and he was old when he came. He had a mate for a while, but she left, then only came back periodically and now hasn't been seen again.

Deaf children swam with Fungi. Disturbed adults and children swam with him. Everyone said that after swimming with Fungi, they couldn't remember to be sad. They could only remember to be happy.

As it happened, a film crew was filming *Far and Away*, a movie about the Irish. Dingle Bay had been cleared for filming. Fungi had gone out to sea, not liking the roar of the helicopters flying overhead. But it was lunch hour and all was still, so Richard and I walked down to the shoreline. Richard told me to take two medium size rocks, put my hands in the water, and knock the stones together. I did as he said, and in a matter of seconds a huge round black nose pushed up between my hands. I HAD MY HANDS ON A DOLPHIN'S NOSE!

Totally unnerved, I screamed and fell backwards from my stooped position onto the hard jagged rocks behind me. Fungi moved out in the water and with his head lying atop the dark sea, waited. I knew what I had to do. Before Richard could stop me, I pulled off everything but my bra and panties and plunged into the water.

I swam out to Fungi and then swam with him. I didn't realize that something unusual was happening until two German men in wetsuits came up to me and asked if I wanted a mask so that I could see everything. I did not need a mask. I could see Fungi even after he dove down into the opaque waters.

I rolled with him as he swam by me and under me and around me. I was weightless. Nothing hindered my body. I was in heaven. I could vaguely hear Richard calling from the shore, but I was oblivious. One of the swimmers said in a thick German accent, *"Lady, you best get in."*

I couldn't. The black, looming water that surrounded my body with a luxurious cold was my private world with this amazing creature. Fungi touched every aspect of my being with his soul. I was home. I was no longer bound by the limited existence referred to as human. I was the being of me, free, expressed now in water, movement, and sound.

The water encased me in close proximity to a being that required no shielding, a being that was pure life, pure love. Fungi's movement was a movement I remembered in the womb of my mother, in the ancient ancestry of my physicality. Sound was *pinging* my cells with multifaceted memories of the beginning of Earth.

I was leaving the fat of my body as I floated in the bay.

A strange thought floated in my mind, "I am leaving the weariness of life that is locked in the traumatized lives of people."

"I am leaving," I suddenly thought.

I then realized that it was true. I was leaving. My body was numb. My heart was slowing down. I was going to sleep right there next to the deep-seated heart of Fungi.

As I realized that my body functions were shutting down, I felt something against me, moving me. Sluggishly, I struggled to go deeper into the water, to drown in its memories. I dropped down into the water with only my head showing and opened my eyes. I was looking right into Fungi's left eye. He lay in the water looking at me… deciding. Then, without warning, he placed his bottle shaped nose in my armpit and swam, pushing me toward the shore.

I was too anesthetized by the cold to fight him. But I wasn't too frozen to not cry. The tears fell down my face. I had met the core of my existence in this exquisite creature, and I did not want to go back to what felt like the sham of human existence. Fungi got me close enough and then backed up and charged me. He hit me straight in my sternum, leaving a bruise, but not breaking anything. It was just enough for my friend Richard to get into the water and drag me to the shore where tea and many blankets awaited me.

I hadn't realized the shore of this inner coastline had become lined with families, teenagers, men and women, and even a couple of priests, watching this woman in her underwear out with their dolphin in their bay. Now they rubbed me down with some kind of warm oil, wrapped me in blankets, and poured Irish black tea down my uncooperative throat. They helped Richard carry me up the hill to where the mossy grass was thick, and I could be laid down to rest. I wasn't allowed to sleep until the local doctor got there and made sure that the hypothermia was not too extreme.

As for me, I wept. I wept and wept and wept. I was halfway between worlds. I was sonar, water, hearing the ocean sounds in my ears combined with the dolphin sounds of kindness. Finally, I was allowed to sleep right there with Richard beside me. People periodically would bring more tea and biscuits (which later I was happy to be addicted to). The movie filming got back underway, and Fungi went out to sea.

I slept for a while, and though I know people would attribute it to the hypothermia, I could feel my cells begin to extend and deepen. My body was changing form even if Richard couldn't see it. I was elongating. As I elongated, a painful ecstasy started at the base of my spine and made its way up my body. The tingling was the body waking from the frozen state it had been in, but under it was memory. There is just no other word for it.

For five hours, I went between ecstasy and agony. My body convulsed either way. I wept both with great joy and great sorrow. Then I rested.

Around dark, Richard took me to where we were to stay. The next morning I felt encased in a creaturehood that extended out beyond the boundaries of my humanity. We left for the ferry. To say the least, the course that weekend was like no other.

When I got home from Ireland after the course, I was in a strange oblivion for about six months. I wandered about the house, not really connected to anything. I dreamed in sonar. As I fell asleep, I would shape-shift out of my body and become a sleek smooth form that moved in the deep seas, using sound waves with a knowledge that required no speaking or thought.

One afternoon, I was sitting out on my lawn behind my condo and my daughter came out and sat down beside me. She said, *"Mama, what are you doing?"* I replied, *"I am listening to the roots of the tree growing."* Somehow those words startled me back into the world I had left behind. Suddenly, I felt reconnected to my family, to my home, and to my human life. Though I would miss my venture into the world of the sea, it was also good to be home.

I swam with Fungi the next three times I went to Ireland. The last day I swam with him, I knew it was the last time. There was just a knowing that came with a fullness of something completely done. I got out of the water, and sat shivering and dripping onshore in the brisk sea breeze, and watched him go out to sea.

Then I heard a name, *Tantra Maat*. It wasn't any name. It was my name. I had no doubt that it was my name, even though at the time I did not know what the name signified. It took me another four years to change my existing name to Tantra Maat. Over time, in my inner awareness, I knew I was embodying the realm of *Tantra* (the union of heaven and earth) and *Maat* (the Egyptian goddess of Truth who weighed the souls of the dead on her scales. If the souls were heavier than a feather, she had to send them back to be born again. Maat wept, so she blindfolded herself so she didn't have to see. She is the forerunner to the United States' statue of Justice).

Being the 'realm of something' is different than being 'someone'. Being the 'realm of something', you begin to operate in a broader awareness about things. You tend to what I call 'the ways of existence itself'. You aren't too interested in human suffering or the human condition (betrayal, abandonment, rejection, and loneliness). And yet, you become more and more capable of impacting life, bringing people into the 'realm of the mysterious and the magical', where dreams can manifest.

Moving into these other 'realms' of existence an entirely new unfolding of life began to occur. I gained more and more awareness of how to bring that to others. Who would have thought that my whole sense of being would be blown apart by a large, imposing, incredibly wise and gentle sea mammal?

CHAPTER THIRTEEN

The Mother Stones

"*What on earth are we doing?*" I thought. We had journeyed to Ballygallen from Cork. Through the dreary weather, the trip had been uneventful. Driving the coastline on a small Irish road is slow, so I was able to see the old-world cottages that dotted the waterline. They were just off the road, down a small hill, nestled against the water's edge.

Irish cottages are so well kept. Flowers dot the ground. The land is allowed to flourish. There is a meld between the land and the property owner. The land isn't tamed, and to look at the yards and the cottages, you would think they had risen together in some kind of perfect order.

Richard had another road trip planned. A client of mine from America had joined us for this outing to a nearby stone circle, an hour and a half away. Even though it only takes three hours to cross Ireland as the raven flies, nothing is really nearby. Everything is convoluted to accommodate the land, the mountains of rock, and the sea.

We stopped on the way for tea at a cheese shop. Oh my goodness! Irish cheese! I still buy Dubliner cheese to this day. It's one of the few Irish cheeses available in my part of the States. The tea tasted strong and hearty (no herbal tea here) with cream, sugar and biscuits. With the sopping rain, we welcomed the comforting warmth.

Over the years, I would stop at this cheese shop again and again. The tables were barrels, set up outside when it wasn't raining. Today, however, we grabbed our tea, stood in the shop and chatted, an art in Ireland. We bought some cheese and soda bread and set off on our adventure.

The rain slid down the windshield in globbed streams, making it hard for the windshield wipers to do any good. Windshield wipers have a hard time in Ireland. I have yet to be in a car where you could see out even with the wipers going full blast. Your instincts and your intuition become very mature when you're driving the roads in Ireland. Either that or you're constantly suffering from panic.

As we got closer to the road that led up to the stone circle, the rain subsided a bit. We decided to stop at the pub at the bottom of the road. The hot tea hadn't lasted very long, so another stop was needed. The small pub was lined with dark wood. A peat fire burned in the hearth. The aroma of the peat and smoke welcomed us and its heat even more so. The bar ran along the back of the wall with benches and small tables in front. I ordered a hot whiskey. If I was going to be out in the rain, I needed fortification.

The rain was only a mist when we left. We wound up the hill until somewhere on the edge of the road, in the middle of nowhere, we pulled over and parked. Oh my! We parked on the outside edge of a really sharp turn with only a small amount of space to get by. I had to trust that Richard knew what he was doing, but I found myself not able to shake my concern.

One of the things I have learned about having 'ways' is that often I will find myself concerned about something that really isn't the source of my concern. It is as though my radar is turning on. With the stiff whiskey in me, tattered from the drive, and the common, casual action of parking so precariously, still uncommon to me, I did not realize that another moment of intrusion into the deepest part of my soul was at hand.

I enjoyed walking the wet, soggy, root-webbed trampoline of bog, even though it wore me out if I went too far. I did not, however, sign up for this sticky wet mud on a cow path up a hill. *"What on earth are we doing?"* I internally demanded.

We struggled up the hill. The cow-trampled terrain was chopped up and slippery, making it hard to know where to step. That, combined with the rain-soaked earth full of cow dung, made the going hard. The mud would suck up my boot, and I would have to stop and literally pull my captured foot up and out of the ground, which was clearly disinterested in my being there.

As we approached the top of what felt like a mountain, though was only a small hill, I realized what on earth we were doing there. In another ten years, you would not be able to come to this array of ancient magic. The farmer would die and his heirs would no longer welcome the seekers of the mysteries. Today, however, as I crested the hill, I saw before me a tall stone monolith. Another stone monolith had been by its side, now fallen. Even with it lying broken on the ground, I could feel that this was a gateway, a ritual passageway into an ancient understanding, perhaps even a dimensional portal into other worlds.

Over to the right, stood a small stone circle. The bottom half of the oval stones were buried in the ground. They were tightly fitted, which is unusual, one stone touching the next. Only the head stone, which was a little bigger, had space enough to walk into the circle. The entire circle was maybe six feet in diameter. I so wanted to enter!

Richard, however, waylaid me to see another treasure... a most ornate faery ring. Farmers in Ireland never damage or destroy a faery ring. This faery ring was a series of circled stones, one circle lying inside another circle, giving the impression of a multi-petaled flower, about four feet in diameter. A small thorny bush was growing in the middle of it.

The power of the place was palpable. Everyone we brought later on also felt it. The farmer had warned Richard about a bull, but neither the bull nor the cows were in sight. Somebody had had the good sense to get in out of the rain.

The small Mother Circle continued to call me. I felt odd. I thought it was the whiskey, but this odd was odder than the effect of a single hot toddy. I walked into the Circle and knelt in front of the larger Mother Stone.

Out in front of me, the sea lay at the end of many inlets and small peninsulas, which were lush, green from the constant rain. The green of Ireland is often referred to, *but it ain't nothin' 'til you see it.* Vibrant greens of every hue contrasted with the pale shimmering blues of the sea and all of it spread out before me.

I felt the impact of some of my personal struggles overwhelm me and tears soaked my cheeks. I grasped onto the Mother Stone, laying my forehead against her cool exterior. I both felt and fought the emotional pain coming up around my all too human mother.

My mother and I loved each other desperately, but when I was twelve my beloved mother succumbed to alcohol. The mother who took me to an astrologer when I was five years old became consumed by the bitterness and helplessness of an alcoholic. The mother, who doted over me, reading to me from, *Psychic Energy, Its Source and Goal,* when I was eight, disappeared.

The loss of my mother surfaced as I gripped the top of the stones with my hands. My heart shuddered with pain as I crumpled into gasping moans. A brief moment of time passed. *Then, as if the Earth Herself were coming to my aid, I felt the ground under me open and embrace me with love. Awareness flooded me. I felt the love of The Mother. The Mother, who gave everything on earth life, would not let me suffer. Remembrance flooded my heart. My mother and I belonged to her. She was our Mother. She cried for us, comforted us, and stood witness to our lives. She was our real Mother.*

I cried out, "You are my real Mother." The comfort I could no longer find in my own mother, I could find here with her. "You are my real Mother!" I cried out again. This time, I lashed out with my head, my forehead hitting the Stone. Again and again, I slammed my head against the Stone, screaming, "You are my real Mother! You are my real Mother! You are my real Mother!"

Years of heartache engulfed me. The yearning for my birth mother crushed me as I beat my head against the Stone.

Spent, I spread face down on the earth, weeping into the ground. The wet ground graciously took my tears.

Then I felt Richard's arms around me, pulling me up against the Mother Stone. His hand was dripping with blood. He had put his hand against the Stone to buffer the impact of the blows on my head.

I vaguely remember wondering if I had broken his hand in my emotional outburst.

Emotional outburst... that is what we would call it in our civilized, modern psychological avoidance of the deepest part of us. Our longing to love. Our passion to be loved. The incredible unreasonable anguish of being without love. I left all that at the Mother Circle that day. I did not break Richard's hand, but he had a bloody bruise for quite a while to mark that day.

We left in silence, holding hands. My client, who was a therapist, was extremely disturbed by the event and wanted to counsel me, but I needed no counseling. The Mother had found me and brought me home to her, where I would always be loved. Not only that, she loved my mother too. I could go home now, not expecting from my mother what she could no longer give. I could go home and love her now. Such is the greatness of The Mother. Such is the profundity of Ireland.

Back at the B&B, covered up in my duvet, hot water bottle cozy at my feet, I felt strange. Much had happened at the personal level for sure. After we left the circle, I felt so relieved. Though still worried that I had damaged Richard's hand for life, I had wandered over to the faery ring and put my head down on the stones before Richard could stop me. He grabbed me and pulled me back, but not before something weird occurred. That was about all there was to it. Something weird occurred. I wasn't sure what, but the weird was still occurring when I got back to the B&B.

Tomorrow, I was taking a train up to Dublin to meet the five High Witches of Ireland for tea. I hoped, as I fell asleep, that the weird would be gone by then.

"There was actually no statute in Ireland criminalizing witchcraft until 1586, sparing Ireland of a plague that took the lives of nearly 50,000 woman and men in the rest of Europe."

—*Unknown source*

CHAPTER FOURTEEN

The High Witches of Ireland

Meeting the High Witches of Ireland is impossible. Unless they ask for you.

How and why they asked for me, I do not understand. How they found Naomi to relay their message to me is unknown. To this day, I still remember her wide-eyed shock and robotic delivery of their message.

A lot of my memory is blank on that day I met them. I do not remember how I arrived or how I left. I now know that the eventful hour at the stone circle the day before was the calling card of the High Witches, and an initiation that prepared me for their scrutiny. It is hard for many to understand how the ancient Druidic mind works.

What we would consider a paranormal or a peak experience is simply part of their daily 'do'. Their daily do is to keep the veils able to part, leading us into other dimensions of existence. Their daily do is to keep portals open for those, like myself, who need to remember who they are beyond their present life chronology. The enduring unity of their earth magic tends toward the netherworlds that live in the molten lava of the earth core, the songs of the whales, the primal forces of the earth, wind, fire, and rain, and the elementals that keep the earth lively and entertained.

I know now that they first felt me through the ethers, rippling across the etheric communication lines into their energy fields, as I met Tom on the knoll and frolicked with the birds and the wind as they responded to my call.

The day I met the five High Witches of Ireland, I was still feeling stoned from the day before. Stoned, not from a hallucinogenic drug, but from being in a direct mind-link with the field of consciousness that dwelled in the circle of Mother Stones that had captured and awakened me.

I still felt strange, weird and wonderful, from laying my head on the faery ring. I was still throbbing from what happened there.

I stood at the door a moment before I knocked. One of the High Witches, the Head Druidess, opened the door. She stood over six feet tall, massive, but not like a fat, fleshy woman you'd see at the mall. She looked as if she was carved from a massive boulder that had come alive. Her eyes pierced into me. I barely survived her gaze as she took in my fleshy five-foot-five body standing before her. I felt like the wayward child who had come to be disciplined by the Mother Superior at the Catholic school.

I am sure she would be insulted by that comparison. I find myself shaky even suspecting she could read my words. The mark of her stays with me, even to this day.

She said nothing and beckoned for me to come in. I entered. She waved me over to a drab, green overstuffed sofa with no legs. I am sure the legs could not have survived her weight. Out of the corner of my eye, I could see four other women sitting having tea. They never looked up to greet me or even acknowledge I was there in any way. All wore long black dresses.

I had seen enough movies to realize I was in a coven. Horror story images jumped into my mind, but their regal appearance and their unspoken command of the space elicited a strange safety in me. At the same time, I also didn't feel safe. I felt ignored, as if I was being tested, but didn't know what I was being tested for.

I could feel a connective webbing of energy that made me aware they were part of the underpinnings that cared for the entire planet. I found safety for the world in that. I wasn't too sure about myself.

I had worn a long dark dress with long sleeves, as I had been instructed. I have never been comfortable sitting in dresses. I held very still, desperately wanting to stare at them.

I was an appropriate adolescent on her best behavior, sitting properly, back up straight, legs together, and hands in my lap, obeying what every child in my era knew: children should be seen, but not heard.

As I sat there trying to figure out how to feel comfortable, I became less and less aware of my physical discomfort and more and more aware of another kind of discomfort. I couldn't feel my bones. I literally could not feel my bones. I closed my eyes to get a grip on reality only to realize reality had become illusive. I opened one eye and peeked at my fingers. The flesh, the muscles were all there, but not my bones. I fought down a severe panic. I hung onto the thought that I was in a paranormal experience. I kept promising myself my bones would eventually return.

I could see why they didn't invite many people over.

As my thoughts whirled around, grabbing at any possible straw of sanity, I felt my spine melt away and my body slumped back against the sofa. There I was, with five women having tea. I was now inserted in the crevice of the sofa. My head flopped over. My entire face went slack. My mouth was open, drooling. My arms were flaccid by my side. I was sliding onto the floor, like a slug, my bones no longer in my legs to hold me up.

Tears poured down my face. I was terrified. I fought to get my mouth moving before I lost my skull. I squeaked out the most inane words, "Please help me. I am only an American!"

That said, I slipped away down a long tunnel filled with a sickening green slimy luminous glow. I was only a mind. But, not only my mind. There was another mind, unfamiliar and intent on taking over my mind. There was nothing I could do about it.

I could feel my body being turned over on its back and stretched out.

The weight of another body was straddling mine and someone else's breath was on my face. I could hear a woman's voice far away from where I was in the dark murky ghost green tunnel. Her voice was stern and commanding, traveling down the tunnel toward me.

"Speak!" she said. Then louder, compelling, "I command you to speak." I couldn't say a word, but the other mind began to grumble and thrash around trying to avoid her command. I knew it was a 'him', a very old 'him'. I knew somehow he had been dormant until now, and he was residing in me (or at this moment I was residing with him).

I was helpless, but she was not. She began to speak in a strange language, and he began to respond.

I could hear women's voices rising in a haunting and convincing cadence, and I was so grateful. The voices vacuumed the tunnel, building suction until the 'being' sharing the tunnel with me was drawn toward them. Then he began to speak through my mouth. He was shouting, as the slime began to undulate around me.

I only remember the first words, "ECK, JOO, BAK" because those were the words that kept coming out of my mouth. I knew they were setting both of us free--that somehow we had gotten tangled up together somewhere. He was intoning in an ancient tongue requesting a primal power to take care of a primal need. I heard her respond to him in the same tongue.

The only way I know how to explain what happened is that he began to understand. There seemed to be a very important exchange of information going on. I seemed to be the vehicle he caught a ride in, to surface for something I did not know. I was clear, even if told, I would not understand. As the strange conversation ended, I experienced such love, such longing coming from him, such veneration coming from them, such gratitude that they were present for whatever had happened, and such joy that it had happened.

Finished, his mind still resting within mine, she began to invoke a spell through a lyrical language. The tunnel began to dissolve. His mind flowed out of mine.

I felt the second he was gone. I opened my eyes with great difficulty, for they still didn't remember how to function. One of the women was wrapping a fist-sized stone pulsing with a green light in a velvet cloth. I could feel her putting it away somewhere. The other four women were kneeling around me rubbing life back into my hands, my feet, and my head. I felt myself come back into form under their care and tending. They were so excited, praising me, chattering away in Gaelic with each other.

The Head Druidess came back over to me and anointed my palms, the soles of my feet, and my brow with oil. She sprinkled water on my forehead and prayed in English.

"Bless this child, Old Mother, who has carried one of the old ones to us this day. We now carry your words from him in our hearts. We will remember."

She ended with a few Gaelic words and then it was over.

"Adam's at the window
Staring at the apple trees on fire
Waiting for the windfall
That brings the smile of kings and their desire"

Adam at the Window'
—Mary Black

ChAPTER FIFTEEN

Meeting Adam

After a few years of working at the Irish Spiritual Centre in Dublin, I had the routine down. I would make my way up the three flights of narrow steps to my turret-like consult room. People would wind their way up the stairs to get consults on their own. I wouldn't have lasted two consults if I had had to go up and down those stairs to get them. I was continually amazed how the Irish, regardless of age, sprang into the room light-footed, still breathing, and ready to go.

After five consults, I would go down the stairs, out the front of the Centre, across the narrow alley and into the shop across the street. Now an Irish 'shop' can be a number of things. A shop can be a place you buy food such as biscuits, which are cookies, or buy necessities such as nappies, which are diapers, or buy clothes such as jumpers, which are sweaters, and knickers, which is underwear. You purchase whatever you purchase and go out and put it into the boot, which is the trunk of your car in the carpark, which is the parking lot. Sometimes, if the shop serves food, there is an area with tables and chairs, which would challenge the occupancy code of any restaurant in the US of A.

This little shop with tables and chairs was literally three steps out the door of the Centre. Once, when I worked late, I got out as the English/Irish soccer match was letting out. As I came down the final stairs and into the street, two garda, which are policemen, were barring my exit. Before I could ask why, a roar of male voices blew down the street. The noise was so loud it sounded like they were being carried by floodwaters. Instinctively, I backed up a few steps to a landing.

Seconds later, a layer of human bodies swept past me with a second layer of live human bodies on top. Fists flew. Men screamed at each other and punched anyone they could find. It looked like a rapidly moving human float with hard core fights on top. Beer bottles and cans flew everywhere. One flew through the door over the garda's head and landed at my feet.

"They're all Brits," the garda said, answering my unspoken question. *"They're a rough lot... been banned from a lot of games."* He was referring to rugby, football, and soccer. I could believe it.

Enraged men were crawling up onto the shoulders of the men below to get in a good punch. Everyone was pressed so tight and moving so fast through the alley that they were literally climbing the walls to avoid being crushed. That was the last night I stayed late during games, especially if the Brits were playing.

The alley, even under normal circumstances, was crowded with people making their way through to the shops. Dodging passersby, I slid into the doorway of the food shop. The routine was to go in, grab a tray, pick up your food, and pay at the counter. Then gingerly make your way to a table.

You learned fast to carry a zippered purse that you could hook in front of you. The tinkers, who were local gypsies, made their pounds by nippin' your valuables. You never saw them. When you reached for your purse, your shopping bag, or your coat, they were simply gone!

Up front, there was a large plate glass window with wooden bars, like a stair railing across it. I was clear it was there to shield the shop from the overly enthusiastic sports fans. I paid for my food in Irish pounds and found a spot up front with my back to the glass. *'The fewer stimuli after a morning of consults, the better'*, I thought. I was so not prepared to be 'stimulated' by the young man, about twenty years my junior, who walked through the shop door.

Now, I love men's butts. My mother finally stopped taking me to the ballet. She was shocked by her six-year-old daughter swooning over the dancers' physiques, especially expressing her enthusiasm for their butts. This young man had one of the most muscular, sensuous asses I had ever seen. Not accustomed to being quite so flushed or turned on, I stared. Thank God his back was turned toward me, so he couldn't see. He was tall, dressed in a black knit tee with short sleeves that showed off the most glorious sun-tanned skin and muscular symmetry. My mouth actually watered.

With his jet-black hair, he was clearly black Irish, the gorgeous mix of Celt and Spanish descent. His muscular shoulders tapered down into a trim belted waist defining his lower torso and legs in an incredibly enticing way. From the rear, he looked like a Greek god that had stepped off his pedestal at the Parthenon and had come out for a stroll.

As cliché as it sounds, the room disappeared and I only had eyes for him. Even in the lunch line, tray in hand, he moved with such primitive sexuality, I was amazed women weren't fainting at his feet. Actually, no one but me even seemed to notice him. He paid for his food, then turned and looked right at me with big, daring, dark eyes. He walked to a table three tables away from me, facing the street, and facing me.

As he leaned over to sit down, I made my escape, leaving the tray of food on the table, untouched. I bolted into the Centre and found myself in my consult room panting profusely (and it wasn't from climbing the stairs). I had a good hour to get myself together by the time my first afternoon client came. I chalked up the experience to a middle-aged woman's mid-life crisis. Something I was not, until that moment, aware I was having. I even smiled and thought, *"Well good! I'm not dead, yet!!"* Launching into the consults with added vigor, I forgot about the incident until right before my last client.

I felt him. I felt him in GREAT BIG NEON LIGHTS pulsing through me.

My last client of the day came, and I fought to stay focused. Thank goodness for thirty years of experience. At the end of the session, with my heart still pounding from the penetration into my psyche, the client said to me, *"There is a young man waiting for you downstairs. He told me not to disturb you until our reading was done. He'd like to see you if you could come down. He even winked at me and said he didn't mind waiting."*

I must have looked like frozen stone because she had to ask me several times if I was all right. I was anything but all right. I dismissed her knowing smile as fast as I could, as thousands of thoughts ran through my mind, *'This is stupid'*, followed by *'This couldn't possibly be 'my' young man'*, intertwined with *'boy, you have some imagination!'*

I packed up, and then worked my way down the stairs. I moved carefully, out of breath, my heart beating in my throat. I hoped he wouldn't know that I was shaking in my knickers.

He didn't even wait until I got to the last step before he was standing one step down, face to face with me, handing me a bouquet of flowers. *"My name is Adam. I think I came to love you."*

Well what do you say? A young, physically fit, enticing Greek god meets a not physically fit over weight middle aged woman on the steps of a spiritual centre and says, *"I think I came to love you."* I don't think anyone has written that script before.

He put the flowers into one of my hands and took my other hand in his. *"Do you have some time right now?"* By now, I was clear that he was a lunatic, and I begged off saying,

"No, I have a public talk tonight and I need to prepare for it."

I had never prepared for a speaking engagement in my life. Once, when I was asked to speak at a women's conference of a thousand women, I stood in the wings and the mistress of ceremonies asked me if I wanted her to put my notes on the podium. When I told her I didn't have notes, she looked at me aghast. I caught my error and said, *"I memorized my speech."* Relieved, she introduced me to the audience for my twenty minute 'speech' that was so well received they asked me to keep going for another hour. So much for notes.

Adam asked me where the talk was and was not the least bit daunted that I had said no. He told me he would meet me there.

A few days before, I had been on a radio show sharing about the shift in the psyche that would occur over the next twenty-five years, from suffering to ecstasy. I spoke of a new freedom that was coming into the hearts and souls of humankind and that even in the amazing chaos that would occur, love would rise in a whole new way. The radio show was a preamble to the talk. I returned to my hotel room, rested, dressed, and headed to where I would be giving the talk.

As I walked into the lobby of the hotel, I was surprised to see it filled with people working their way to the elevator to hear the American woman talk. I love the Irish. Letting someone in the crowd know I was the American woman, and I needed to get to the room, the red sea of humans parted. I even rode up on the elevator alone.

As I came out of the elevator, I was met by the hotel manager who let me know that their largest room held 70 people and that there were already 90 there. I was both delighted and worried. Then, just like in the movies, the elevator door opened with more people and in front of them was Adam. *"What's the problem?"* he asked looking at my creased brow. *"There isn't enough space for everyone in the room,"* I replied. Taking my arm in a gentlemanly way, sweeping me across the hall, he laughed and said, *"Oh yes there is! This is Ireland."*

I don't know what he said to people, but everyone responded. I was installed at the front of the room. Chairs were taken out. People sat on the floor all around me. Others lined the walls. There was not an ounce of extra space anywhere, yet it did not look crowded at all. We stopped the flow of people at a whopping one hundred and twenty.

A thin aisle started at my feet and ran to the back of the room so people could get in and out. As I started speaking, I realized Adam was at the back of the room directly facing me, sitting on the floor, his back against the wall, his elbows resting on his knees, beaming his beautiful smile and sparkling eyes at me.

I didn't have any problem talking about the shift from suffering to ecstasy that evening.

"Set them free, no matter what they say
Set them free, for they live another way
It's the Spirit of the Wild Things
That you love so much to see
But wild, wild things can turn on you
And you've got to set them free"

Lyrics from 'Wild Things'
—Cris Williamson

CHAPTER SIXTEEN

A Day at the Zoo

From that night until I left to go back to the States three weeks later, Adam and I were inseparable.

I never asked him why he was drawn to be with me or I was drawn to him. I never once thought it was so he could come to the States or because he was taking advantage of me. He paid his own way and was his own man. There was something else, something much larger and deeper that occurred between us.

As I have continued to do the work I do, I realize that we all long to be recognized for who we truly are. Why? Without being seen as what we truly are, something foundational is missing. We are run by fear. When we know who we are, we trust our choices. Risk is easier because what we are risking is based on the strength and clarity that comes from that deep self- knowledge. That is what brought Adam and me together. We not only recognized each other as who we truly were beyond appearances, age, or country, we were able to share what we recognized in our connection.

I loved that Adam was exquisitely formed and extraordinarily handsome. It wasn't an ego thing. He was a world I remembered. I had been with that amazing type of being in Adelphi when I was an oracle and he was a philosopher and an athlete. I remembered the statues of the gods and how they emulated perfection. I was home.

This world had not been an easy place for him. He had struggled with drink as a teenager. He was incredibly strong. Until he got sober, he would sometimes jump from the second floor of a building or turn over a car or two. He loved sunlamps and could not get enough sun, soaking in the rays of the lamp until he was roasted.

Adam was not like anyone else. Neither was I. The bond was ancient and unrelenting, based on a desire to know a world that eluded us in our modern day lives. The powerful urge to know who we truly are was not as prevalent back then as it is now. Now after all these years, more people are awakening, struggling with the possibility of really knowing who they are, and in that knowing, courageously taking on the search to find a place for themselves.

Adam had a single room flat in Clonsilla. We would go there and just be. Sometimes we would simply fall asleep.

He would be in his shorts, and I would have my head on his hip, and we would fall asleep in front of the fire. One evening I woke up and started laughing. I woke him up with my laughing, and he asked me what was so funny. I told him that he had ruined any story I had about who I could be with. A large American woman almost twenty years his senior, resting her head on the hip of an Irish Greek Adonis. It made a great story.

He took what I said very seriously however. He stood up and lifted me up to my feet in a most gentlemanly way. My nose was right at his Adam's apple. He tilted my chin and looked right into my eyes and said, *"I already know my beauty outside. You already know your beauty inside. We are a perfect match! I will learn my inner beauty that you see, and you will learn your outer beauty that I see."*

I couldn't help but smile.

Adam loved clothes. Whenever we decided to go out, he would ask me what I thought of what he was wearing. I would always suggest he should try on something else. Sometimes, I could make it an hour with Adam changing into many outfits before he realized I didn't care what he wore. I just liked watching him model for me!

Even though we spent long hours together, often late into the evening, I always went back to where I was staying. It just seemed right.

One day, Adam suggested we go to the zoo. He met me at the centre dressed in black, form-fitting jeans, with a white knit, short sleeve tank. I was dressed in something not form-fitting and quite non-descript. We caught a taxi and off we went.

The taxi meandered through Phoenix Park, one of the largest walled city parks in Europe, until a tall obelisk, the Wellington Monument, came into view. Getting out at the Dublin Zoo, Adam held my hand and started walking so fast I had to skip to keep up. It was good to be out in the fresh spring air and to have the whole day ahead of us.

Our first mutual choice was the wolves. If there is an animal Adam and I once were, it is definitely a wolf. A lot of our private time in the future would be much more in keeping with the wolf pack, rather than the social strategies of human beings.

I saw the grey, sharp-eyed female wolf first, before I got to the cage. The rush of feeling I get from connecting with wild animals is so potent, sometimes the hairs on my body get electric. I feel so alive being with them.

I walked straight up to her, and sat cross-legged on the ground in front of her. Adam squatted down beside me. He watched the male wolf at the back of the den. The wolf raised his head and looked at Adam. They watched each other for some time. Finally, the male wolf joined us. Adam and I then got on all fours, our noses almost touching the chain link fence. The wolves moved their noses almost touching the fence. I could feel the she-wolf's breath, and I knew she could feel mine. We stayed eye-to-eye with these majestic creatures a long time.

Pretty soon, a little boy in his Catholic Sunday best tiptoed over to me. I could see him out of the corner of my eye, fascinated by the two wolves standing nose-to-nose, very still, linked to these two humans. As the boy made his way quietly towards me, other children began to sit down around us, in silence, knowing with the intelligence of a child something was afoot.

The ruddy, red-haired little boy brushed my ear with his lips, as he whispered, *"Who are you? Who is he?"*

The spellbound moment of wolf and human melted as the wolves stepped back, and returned to pacing the parameters of their cage. When I visited the zoo after that day, I never saw them stop again, to be eye-to-eye with another human being.

The fantasy-filled air lingered, and into that I said, as I turned toward the children, *"Have you ever heard of Jack and the Beanstalk?"*

I realized it was not a traditional Irish faerytale, when all the children and the couple of mothers with strollers (in Irish, called "trams"), shook their heads, *"No."*

I launched into a story about Adam. *"Do you see that man, right here beside me? He just escaped from this big giant in the sky."* I had their attention. Adam chimed in, *"Right, and you wouldn't believe how I got here."* And off we went creating our own fable of who Adam was, and how I came to find him.

We had gotten up, and the children were gleefully skipping along beside Adam, keeping up with his long-legged stride, as on and on the tale kept spinning.

"And, the lady I am with," Adam said, *"is a guardian of the crea-*

tures of a forest in a faraway place from here. She was visiting her forest when I came sliding down the big tree, escaping from the giant. She was crying because someone had taken some of her animals and brought them here. I came with her to make sure they were okay," he announced as we stopped in front of the largest, most orange orangutan I had ever seen. *"Then I began to cry too."*

The orangutan was sitting on the grassy ground right behind the high fence, shelling and eating peanuts. I watched as Adam squatted down, looking like an elegant black and white grasshopper, his long legs poking up in front of him. The orangutan, still shelling his peanuts, began to flip the peanut shells at Adam. Adam kept smiling and gathering them up, as the orangutan kept shelling them and flipping them.

Adam, hand bulging with shells, picked one shell out, and flicked the shell with his nail through the chain-linked fence … ZAP! Right onto the orangutan's nose. That got the up-until-then rather bored ape's attention.

The orangutan burrowed his eyes into Adam's eyes, as one shell after another zapped him. Calmly, the orangutan began methodically to gather the shells up, until some of the shells were sliding out of his grip. With his other hand, he picked up a shell, and flicked it back at Adam with his long hairy finger. With lightening speed, the shell bulleted into Adam's nose.

I was a wreck, watching out for any zookeeper in the area, as well as worried we were going to have an enraged ape on our hands. I had lived in Saudi Arabia where orang-utans were feared. They were fierce fighters, and got pissed off for no apparent reason tearing the flesh off of their opponent, with their shell-cracking teeth. This orangutan was much older than the other testosterone males that could steal babies and pick fights. Maybe that would make a difference, I hoped.

Adam and the orangutan were really getting into their shell fight. People had come from all over to watch, and the kids around Adam were hopping with excitement. Adam was bouncing around on his feet like a pogo stick, knees bent like a Russian dancer. The orangutan was swinging on the ropes, running zigzag across the grass-floored cage, a seasoned fielder popping shells at Adam from everywhere.

The kids were running around gathering up the ammunition for Adam. We were all laughing. Adam finally rolled onto his knees, looked up at the frolicking grandfather ape, folded his hands in prayer, laughed and said, *"I give up."*

It took a minute for the orangutan to stop his shell fight strategy. Finally, he came back to his original spot, and bored again began shelling and eating peanuts.

In true Irish fashion, the story was savored, each person sharing their version. Adam was patted on the back profusely, *"Good show! Simply grand! Awesome!"* He was exhausted. We needed to eat.

By then, we had an entourage of about ten children and their mothers, who decided it was time for them to eat too. We all bought our fresh-wrapped sandwiches at the shop, got a soda, and sat down on the grass, unintentionally, at least for Adam and me, in classroom fashion. Adam and I faced the mothers and children, and the children and mothers faced us.

In between keeping our tall tale going with the kids, and now the mothers who had joined in, and getting ready to leave, it took me a minute to recognize that the orange flash in the corner of my eye was the orangutan.

I whirled away from looking at Adam, and looked out across the field, only to see the orangutan out of his cage, rushing towards us.

The orangutan was half a football field away, coming fast. Three zookeepers were coming from every direction, trying to intercept him. I knew the danger. If any of the kids tried to touch him, they could lose an arm. The mothers gasped.

I put my finger to my mouth and in a loud whisper said, *"Shhhhhh!"* Then again really, really loud, as loud as I could, again and again, *"Shhhhhhhhh! Shhhhhhhhh! Shhhhhhhhh! Lie down on the ground, face down, now! Don't move! Tuck your arms under your chest!"*

The mothers practically landed on top of their children, long-legged mothers covering over their young ones in their frightened nest. Just in time, as the orangutan ran between them, right into Adam's arms. I slapped my hand over my mouth to keep from crying out.

Adam sat absolutely still. The zookeepers strategically got into place to somehow retrieve their escaped inmate. Adam closed his eyes tight as the orangutan rummaged through his hair, looking for lice. The orangutan seemed to be fascinated with Adam, picking at his sweater, pulling his ears and nose, actually, quite content to be curled up on his lap.

One of the zookeepers said to Adam, *"See if you can stand up."*

Adam kept his eyes still closed and unfurled his grasshopper legs with the orangutan hanging on in a slow, well-orchestrated dance. As Adam stood, the orangutan slipped down to the ground and placed his long-fingered, furry hand into Adam's hand.

"Follow me," the zookeeper said, moving well out in front of the two unexpected companions.

The other two zookeepers moved behind, also keeping their distance.

Bobbing little heads and eyes kept peeking out, and then turning back, sticking their faces into the ground. *"Everyone stay still,"* I whispered. One of the men smiled at me in thanks.

As soon as Adam and his novel friend had gone a distance, the kids' moms and I turned to get a full watch. The two of them were walking just alike, loose-legged ancestors headed out of sight.

The next day, early in the morning, I went to the train to meet Adam. He wasn't there. I went back to the B&B to make breakfast before I went back to see if he was on the later train.

When I came into the room, people were laughing at the television. There, in clear view, were Adam and I, nose-to-nose with the wolves, then a clip of the shell fight with the orangutan, ending with Adam and the ape walking back to his cage together. The local TV station had been at the zoo to film: 'A Day at the Dublin Zoo'.

"Oh nothing can help
The full heart that's breaking
Won't find the words
And you can't hide the feelings
And it's down to bone
To the heart of the matter
You're free free as stone
You're free free as stone "

'Free as Stone'
—Mary Black

CHAPTER SEVENTEEN

Bring the Stones Home

It was time to go back to the USA again. So much had happened. I was so different now. Ireland had taken me out of my modern adaptation of life and brought me into the ancient mysteries that concrete sidewalks and busy schedules conceal. I had come to Ireland completely unprepared for what I found. I had found home. Now boarding the big jet to carry me across the Atlantic, I settled into a middle seat in the center of the plane.

It was one of those large planes that have three seats on each side and six in the center. The plane was crowded, largely with Irish traveling across the Atlantic to New York City and beyond. In the early 1800's, the population of Ireland rose to eight million. With the potato blight that followed, and the penal laws enforced by the British government, over a million Irish immigrated to the United States. By the end of the 1800's, the population of Ireland was reduced by three million and has stayed that way pretty much until today.

We were nearing St. Patrick's Day, a well-celebrated Irish festival and New York City is a great place to celebrate. Irish families filled most of the plane.

I felt ambivalent on that flight back to the USA. I had found a powerful kinship with the Irish, and the land had welcomed a 'me' that I had felt but never known.

Somehow, going back to the Washington D.C. area was like going back to a pretend life with no real juice to it. I settled into sleep as I flew a red eye home. All the lights were out on the plane, the soft purrs of the sleeping passengers filled the air all around me.

I passed into a peaceful oblivion only to be awaked by a powerful voice inside my head ordering me to 'bring the stones home'. Then I heard my own voice shouting in the dark, "What do you mean bring the stones home?!" As I jolted awake, all I could imagine in my half asleep state was how impossible it was going to be to load those monoliths of stone onto a plane. Lights came on all around me, some calling the flight attendant to quell my brutal interruption of their sleep.

I was sweating. The images and thoughts of struggling to get the gigantic stone monoliths of Ireland into the baggage compartment underneath the plane disturbed me all the way home. I continued to be in a constant state of disquiet until I returned again to Ireland a year later.

Returning home was more traumatic than I had imagined. When I landed in New York City, I was taken aback by the rudeness of everyone there. It was so different from the jovial, light-hearted welcome of strangers when I touched down in Dublin. I got a train down to Washington, DC and could not help but notice the weariness of the passengers, slumped over, their heads down, their eyes plastered to a book or a newspaper. No chatting amongst the strangers here. No cheery laughter bubbling over the benches of the train. No children running up and down the aisles, welcomed by the other passengers.

I was struck by the thought that the United States of America suffered from a real spiritual deprivation. In Ireland, there was a spiritedness, yet not in a religious or a New Age spirituality way. In Ireland, there was a powerful, direct relationship with the source of life itself. As I watched people avoid each other's eyes, I wondered if when we left our original homelands to come to America, we lost the roots that gave us our spirit. Were we the rootless, living in an adopted country, separated from ancestors who we had long forgotten?

Is this why we were strangers to each other? Had we, in our high priced clothes, with our leather briefcases, and our 'well-behaved' children, found a good life, but in finding that life, lost the juice of life itself?

In Ireland, the stones were the ancient unforgotten templates of existence that held life for weary Westerners whose roots had been torn out of their souls while trying to survive modern civilization.

I realized, as I sat looking around me, that we all looked like stones--lifeless, out of sync with life, disconnected from the land. *'Bring the stones home' rang out again in my thoughts. Then I knew! I was to bring people to Ireland, people from the United States of America. I was to put their feet onto the land. I was to bring them to The Mother, turn them over to her and let her teach them to remember the same way she had taught me.*

In the four-hour train ride back home, I constructed my first trip to Ireland. I decided to bring healers, people who had some ability to connect into the deeper essences of life. I wanted to bring people with depth so I didn't have to deal with a touristy trip. That was the last thing I wanted.

The most important thing was that the statement *'bring the stones home'* made sense now. Yes, a mystical sense, but sense nonetheless. We were the stones that had been taken from our homes because of fear, poverty, prejudice, or many other factors that made us leave our roots and come to a new land.

Ireland carried a deep-rooted connection between the people and the earth. In my beautiful, progressive, affluent country we had lost touch with our roots to the earth and to each other. In losing touch with those connections, we had become afraid. We did not trust the ground under our feet. We had no real sense of community or hospitality as a nation. We were the rugged individualists who prided ourselves on being self-made men and self-made women.

We had no shared experience of connection because we were all disconnected from the mysterious relationships that are fundamental to the security of a human being. We had been cut off from the mysteries, delegated to a frenetic world of hurrying and scurrying, doing all the things we thought we had to do to have all the things we thought we had to have.

Riding on that train going back to my suburban house in Virginia, I knew that if I could just put people on the land, have them slog the bog, get drenched by the pissin' rain, and be charmed by the lilt of Irish laughter, humor, and hospitality, they would be stones that had come home. They would find their place in the scheme of things. They could find their place on this Earth that loves us.

Maybe the people I brought would be welcomed by the faeries and taunted by the leprechauns. And most importantly, maybe they would be haunted by the mysterious forces that build the muscle for life in human beings. Ireland could bring them a strength of experience that could make them fearless in their daily lives and 'tuned in' to what fulfilled them.

By the time I got home, I was excited. I was even imagining what it would be like to have my fellow passengers there -- the stiff black-suited business man with his leather briefcase or the young gaunt woman, eyes down, looking at nothing in the seat opposite me. What about the livelier bohemian in his thirties, bitter that he could not be enjoyed for his eccentricities? Yes, someday I would bring these stones home. But for now, I would start with the people I felt would be the most able to receive the gift of the mysteries.

BOOK TWO
THE QUEST

CHAPTER EIGHTEEN

Preparing for the Quest

I was ready. I would take a week to travel. The Mother would guide me. I knew that the first trip to Ireland, the first Irish Vision Quest, would rise to meet me. I was driven by an urge that would soon have me roving through the countryside as the framework of what the journey was to be, materialized.

After traveling to Ireland all those years, the voices of the land talked to me. It was that simple. The time had arrived. I was to bring Americans to Ireland. I was to 'bring the stones home'.

How would I design a trip to fulfill a command to 'bring the stones home'? I didn't know, but I was about to find out.

I needed a car so I could meander through Southern Ireland's countryside. I rented the car in Dingle, which was not as crowded as Dublin. I had a huge seafront carpark to practice driving in before I took off on the back roads.

I had not driven since the day I rented my first car in downtown Dublin many years before. Downtown Dublin is a series of narrow roads that press against stone buildings with not a trace of a shoulder. I had just gotten off the plane and had that strange disassociation that comes with jet lag. The world was wavy, not quite solid.

At that time, the rental office was in town so I took a taxi into Dublin, checked into my B&B and crashed for ten hours. The next morning, I awoke not quite refreshed, but no longer feeling like I was going to black out if I had to take one more step. I grabbed a bus at the nearest stop, glad to have the exact change, something I had conquered several years before, after finally figuring out pence, pound, and coin. Getting out near the rental agency, I was shocked to realize it was tucked in the middle of a busy narrow street that went both ways.

Not to be dissuaded. After all, what could be so hard? It was just the opposite side of the street that I would be driving on.

I picked the smallest, reddest, shiniest car I could see, that most importantly, pointed right at the entrance into the street. I wanted the most uncomplicated way to maneuver the narrow crowded streets. It was important for me to be visible.

When I got in the car, I was horrified to discover it was manual. I asked if there were any automatics. The rotund clerk, who a minute before had been affable, stopped, looked at me as if I were demented, and said, *"No."* I was shocked. I thought, *"What were the rental companies thinking, to allow tourists, who have never driven on the 'wrong' side of the road, to drive a stick?!"*

I opened the right side of the car and got in. The passenger seat had a steering wheel. *"Oh! My! G__!"*

Sniveling, I thought, *"Manual drive, can you believe it? And I'm sitting in the passenger side of the vehicle. What if I hadn't learned to drive a stick in the States?!"*

I tried to soothe my nerves, *"No big deal!"*

My mind screamed, *"Yeah! Big deal!"*

My left hand, not my right, would be shifting gears. And even though my left foot would still be working the clutch and my right foot would be on the brake and the gas, trying to put it together, *"Never!"*

Cautiously, I got my feet and hands placed in their appropriate positions. I practiced several times without starting the car, but I was all screwed up. My left hand had not been trained to do what my right hand had trained for. My brain shut down, crossed its wires, and withdrew from any level of participation, not the least bit interested in computing this new way of doing things.

It didn't help that I had been driving an automatic for the last ten years. There was no way I could back up. Reverse was push down, shift far left, and pop up. It just wasn't going to happen. Grateful I chose a car facing the exit, I intended to only drive forward.

I had the audacity to think that Ireland had a system of main highways in the early 90's. I thought if I could get out onto the main highway, I could coast along, not having to deal with much more than fifth gear. I was so wrong.

I rolled toward the exit, putting the car in first very carefully.

First gear in place, I started the car and drove forward just enough to push the clutch back into neutral and cleverly coast over the exit bump. Cautiously, I rolled into the street. Horrified, I realized I was going to have to cross over traffic to turn right to get to where I was going.

Right was not my normal right. Right was all the way over on the other side of the street. I stalled. The Irish drivers on both sides of the street stopped at once. Some ingrained instinct signaled them. *"Some bloody tourist is trying to drive out of a rental agency carpark again!"*

I ground the gears trying to get the car to move again. Nothing is harder than trying to get a car in gear when it feels like the entire population of Ireland is staring at you.

Finally, first gear caught. I turned right into the space on the left side of the road provided me by the miffed but polite drivers.

Turn complete. I decided I was not going to try to shift into second. Creeping along at a snail's pace, whatever confidence I felt evaporated. The cow-path-sized street was lined on both sides with parked cars. For the most part, Irish automobiles are small, but it doesn't make any difference, their streets are small too.

"Praise the Lord! I bought all the possible damage coverage I could, including hitting a sheep!"

What I hadn't prepared for was the possibility of damage happening so soon. Crunched between parked cars with cars coming towards me, I entered a kind of fear-induced trance. Keeping the nose of the car pointing straight ahead, I squinted at oncoming traffic, opening my eyes just long enough to give my car gas so it could skinny past the next oncoming auto.

All this was well and good, except for the horns blaring from behind me. I was mortified by my cowardice, but given the level of fear I was experiencing, I'd deal with my humiliation later.

It wasn't until I came upon a roundabout that things fell apart. A roundabout is a circular section of road that is entered into from two or more side streets. In the early 90's, there were no directional arrows painted on the asphalt, so it was pretty much every man or woman for him or her self. I had no choice except to drive right into it. I swear the fellow behind me would have rear-ended me if I hadn't kept driving.

I blanked out and couldn't remember whether to turn left or right. The road I needed next was on the left, so I erroneously figured, in my now moronic state, that the shortest distance between the two points was the key. So I idled left.

That done, in a split second I realized that the autos entering from all the three other roads were coming straight at me.

I gunned it now, clutch grinding into 4th gear, missing 2nd and 3rd. The red indicator shot over into the 'change gears' margin. The car left the road, crossed the sidewalk, and stalled on the front lawn of a large Catholic church.

The beatific face of a white carved statue of Mother Mary looked peacefully down at me, even though my fender was a foot away from her pedestal.

A priest, his black cassock fluttering in the breeze, hurried out and kindly asked me if I was okay. Sobbing like a baby, I apologized for almost running into Mother Mary.

Several cars drove into the church carpark, which I missed completely, to check on me. No one seemed at all upset I had almost caused a massive auto pileup. One of the men, unconcerned that the auto was in my name only, hopped in the car and drove it over the well groomed lawn and parked it more appropriately in the carpark.

Flustered, I asked the priest if I could leave the car there. I had to go back to the rental agency to turn the car in. Several people offered me a ride but the thought of getting in a car again was nauseating. I walked all the way back to the rental company which actually wasn't that far, given I wasn't driving much faster than a brisk walk. I walked in the door of the agency, plunked the key down on the counter, told them where the car was parked, and asked them to call me a taxi back to my B&B. They did not seem the least surprised or disturbed.

Now I was different. I knew 'Irish time'. Irish time is simple---it is all the time in the world. I had all the time in the world to drive around in circles at the carpark by Dingle Bay, grinding gears to back up and go forward while the locals smiled and made good neighborly fun. They even gave me tips on how to manage the road out of Dingle.

I went pale when a young newly licensed teen was telling me how to keep from stalling out, driving up O'Connor Pass. O'Connor Pass would never be on my driving itinerary. Driving it was only for the brave, though it was one of my favorite places outside of Dingle.

When I worked in Cork, I would take a few days during my busy consult schedule to come to Dingle. A taxi man would drive me half way up the O'Connor pass. I would bring my raingear and a backpack and find a cushy spot on the steep side of the hill overlooking Dingle Bay. I once took a picture every fifteen minutes for four hours. No two pictures were the same. The colors would go from bright green to masked hazy greens, to a dark blue sky threatening rain, to a pale blue sky streaked with wispy clouds, making the ocean and the sky appear as one. Everyone I showed the pictures to, had no idea they were looking at only one view. The landscape changed that much.

Once, I fell asleep and jolted awake. A mountain goat was chewing on my hair. I didn't know who was more shocked -- me sliding down the hill to get away from him or him bounding up the mountain side to get away from me.

When I left the Dingle carpark, I was going to drive up narrow, path-like roads with miles and miles of stone walls lining both sides. Around noon, I headed out. The forces I had acclimated to over the years were taking me out for a jaunt. I felt it as I traveled the back roads past pristinely kept homes, with a pub and a church in every village. I drove until there were no houses.

Out in the middle of nowhere, two things happened at once. The exceptionally bright blue clear sky disappeared into rolling black clouds, pregnant with rain. And then my car died. The moment the car died, the heavens opened up and all around me gushers of water flooded the road. Since I had no way to contact anyone, I sat in the car waiting for the rain to end. I waited until it was almost dark.

The rain, still coming, had reduced to a steady stream of water but not enough to blind me. I got out of the car and headed for the brightest lights I could see in the distance that I could walk toward without leaving the road. As I walked toward the lights I realized I was looking at a couple of farmhouses near the edge of the bay. I headed for the closest one.

Soon the steady stream of water became gushing rain again, drowning my clothing and drenching me. The rain was so heavy I could hardly see a thing and dark was coming fast. With the sky now closed off from the sun, I squished my way across a farmyard to a door.

I banged on the door with my teeth chattering. An elderly man answered. Dressed in a high neck ClanAran sweater, covered by a worn overcoat, his face aged from both weather and years, he greeted me in Gaelic.

It didn't take me long to realize that he spoke no English. He beckoned me in, chatting away, clearly unconcerned that we had no verbal commonality. He motioned me to a back bedroom and pulled out an oversized bathrobe that had seen a lot of years. He took my windbreaker and left. I got the message. I stripped down, put on the worn robe, slid my shriveled feet into way too big slippers, carried my clothes out to the roaring fire and hung them next to my windbreaker on the chairs he had put out for me. The fireplace was an old cooking fire pit, large and imposing, with a mini bonfire going strong.

He settled down with his pipe. I tucked myself into a big armchair, worn from children romping on its fat cloth arms. The seat was sunken in from much use over goodness knows how many years. It was the perfect seat for someone as cold as I was. And it was close enough to the fire that I could get warm.

I was staring at the fire, avoiding the old man's eyes. Bushy eyebrows overhung deep set eyes with thick eyelashes, white now with strips of what once had been that rich black hair of Spanish descent. While I was watching the fire, the old man was watching me. I wasn't uncomfortable at all being in the room with him. I was uncomfortable at the thought of staring back at him.

I had a pang of wishing that I was as comfortable in my skin as he was. I would have loved to be able to stare at people unabashedly just because they were there, a new oddity in the magical world of storytelling. I realized that it was useless to try to figure out what I was going to do while the rain was claiming every inch of space outside of this large farmhouse. Then he began to speak Gaelic right at me. I had to look at him.

I made myself settle in and listen, working to look at him as fully as he was looking at me. Luckily, I find Gaelic is exquisite to hear. On and on he went, building with excitement, shaking his head clearly perplexed, and then indicating that something was finally settled. What he was excited about, what perplexed him and what got settled, were completely absent from my understanding.

After drawing in a deep, satisfying breath from his pipe, he started up again. The night carried on. I still had no idea what I was going to do. My clothes were far from dry, and here I was in a house with an old man, alone. Yet, somehow it all seemed fine.

I did not have a clue what he was talking about, but I was not bored, in fact I was completely engaged. I almost cried at one part of the story and didn't know why. After a while, I realized he was telling the same story almost word for word over and over. There is an old saying, 'the story is in the tellin'. No kidding! This is one of the fundamental principles of chatting in Ireland, you pretty much tell the same story over and over, enjoying the juice of it, never running out of fascination as you tell it. I gotta tell you. He must have told the same story well over ten times. And it wasn't a short story.

Finally, around the eighth time, I began to get the picture. Don't ask me how I did that, but the story began to form in my mind through his repetition. I figured out he had lost one of his sheep near the cliffs of Dingle and that he had searched day and night for it. That had been when I almost cried…his loyalty to his four-legged animal. It wasn't about the money, it was about true ownership. It was never okay for an Irish farmer to lose a sheep.

Sometimes fathers and sons even lost their lives while climbing the high mountains to find their lost animals. As the fog of thinking that words were the source of understanding lifted, I realized he had lost his sheep down a hole, near a sheer drop-off along Dingle Bay. He had heard the sheep baaing and had gone back to find men to help him get it out of the hole. While I didn't get the full details, it wasn't hard for me to fathom that it had been quite something to get that sheep out of that hole and up to the surface.

The last part I never quite got, but I could feel his deep heartfelt joy at rescuing his sheep. The tenor of his voice shook just a bit letting me know it would have been a great tragedy for him if he had lost his sheep that day. Satisfied that the story had been told, he ushered me to the bedroom I had changed in. Without a thought, I curled up in the chill of the room, under the thick covers, warmed by the story of a man and his sheep.

"May the road rise up to meet you, may the wind be ever at your back.
May the sun shine warm upon your face and the rain fall softly on your fields.
And until we meet again, May God hold you in the hollow of his hand."

—An Irish Blessing

CHAPTER NINETEEN

Finding Con

I woke the next morning to the farmer's daughter, surrounded by her flock of tiny children, making breakfast. Her husband had gone to pick up my car. After breakfast, he would pick up his wife, the kids, and me so I could get another car.

Traveling back an entirely different way, through small populated towns and abandoned famine villages, I saw the Blasket Islands. They rested alone surrounded by ocean off the coastal road to Dingle. The minute I saw them, I knew I wanted to bring people there. I thought to camp, a very popular American tradition, yet uninteresting to most Irish.

Once in town I asked around, looking for a guide, hopefully one who would camp, but to no avail. Frustrated, I picked up my new rental and headed back to Cork. On the way, I saw a sign for the Gap of Dunloe. Attracted, feeling the call, I headed for the Gap.

The Gap of Dunloe, Bearna an Choimín in Irish, is a wide crevice between the Macgillycuddy's Reeks and the Purple Mountains near Killarney. Around the town of Killarney I drove past the British built estates, tree-cleared with manicured lawns and properly planted gardens inside. I could taste the bitterness of history. I could feel the disdain for the Irish and the enforced poverty beside the opulence of the landowners that had taken their land. I felt a chill from the blight on the Irish soul.

Everything shifted as I came into the mouth of the Gap of Dunloe. I parked in front of a small Irish farmhouse, Kate Kearney's Cottage, a full on Irish pub. Stone floors with small brown low wooden tables and benches took me out of the modern age into the timeworn hospitality of the Irish. *"Good Day to you, my Lady! What will you have today?" "A fine pint of Guinness hits the spot!"*

The one-sided conversation persisted without the pub owner's need for me to take part. I had no ability whatsoever to decline the offered Guinness, even knowing the irrevocable haze that would overcome me soon after.

This is one of many things I treasured about Ireland. Their gab. Their stories. I hadn't done bars for many years in the US. Bars in my country of birth were often hosted by the gods of distraction and seduction. Here in Ireland, the gab, the talk, the laughter was the heart of life itself, warming my blood not with testosterone but with inclusion. The heart of hospitality twinkled my dulled eyes and burst open my lips and I laughed in spite of myself.

I had left behind the notion of camping in the Blasket because I couldn't find anyone who would take me there. Now in the Gap of Dunloe, staying focused on my mission though hazed by the foam of the Guinness, I asked about camping in the Gap. It turned out that the entire Gap was owned by the Moriarty family and their neighbors. The father, mother and daughter owned and ran the only clothing store down the road.

Arriving at the store, I was overcome by the linens, the intricately knitted sweaters, and the colorful blankets folded neatly everywhere. The memory of meeting Mr. Moriarty still warms my heart today. I could have been a long lost relative the way he took me in. He told me I should talk to his son Con, who did guided tours out of Dingle. I immediately called from the store and left a message and headed back to Dingle.

Following the convoluted meandering indicative of a quest, I got there as The Mountain Man shop was closing. Con wasn't there.

Ready to go back to Cork, I knew a link had been forged for the Quest. I drove to where I could see the Blaskets, parked my car, stood by the stone wall protecting me from the cliff and watched the sunset. *"Thank you,"* I whispered.

I never spoke to Con before I left Ireland. I had a fax address so when I got home, I sent him a fax describing the trip I wanted to take. I will never forget the fax I got in return. He said very clearly that what I had suggested would not accomplish what I wanted to achieve. Then he outlined his recommendations.

Con suggested what I would have asked for if I had known. In that first fax, he stirred the underpinnings that had engaged me ever since I came to Ireland. What he described was way beyond a tourist tour. I knew he listened to what I needed someone to hear. I knew he could hear the deeper current of life that had invited the forces I heard in the plane to tell me to plan this quest.

"Who is this man? How does he know what I need to achieve?"

"Is he really listening to what I am listening to?"

"Are the forces really talking to him?"

Planning the quest with Con was a journey in itself. Mostly we faxed back and forth, but once, needing to discuss the final details of the trip, I called him.

The wind roared as he answered his cell phone. Behind him, I could hear someone shouting. When Con turned for a moment to hear what that someone was saying, the wind stopped and I heard, *"Con, get off the fooking phone!"*

As the wind began roaring into the cell phone again, I shouted, *"Where are you?!"*

"I am holding a rope for my friend Mick here. We are climbing up a wild sea cliff near the tip of Dingle," he yelled back.

I quickly told him I would call later.

126

Finally the day arrived. I came to Dingle a few days before the journey began, to meet Con and ride with him in what would be our cherished minibus, to pick up Adam and then the 'participants'.

It was early June 1992. He was coming to pick me up at the B&B he had arranged for me. I had been coming to Ireland since 1989, starting in Dublin. I had then been invited to Cork and now here I was, getting ready to have others hear the siren song of Ireland and be lured into her lair.

I waited for him to arrive.

As I heard him thump on the door to have the owner come and get me, the calm of the ancient land came over me and I remembered. I didn't try to figure out what I remembered. I remembered him. That was all I needed to know.

And as I remembered, I smiled.

"Together we
Together you see
Together free
Together we"

Clannad Lyrics, Together We
—P.Brennan

CHAPTER TWENTY

Con and I Remember

I felt shaken as I watched Con. I thought of the Irish blessing, *'may the road rise up to meet you'*. The Irish earth rose up to meet him. I could feel how at home he was in nature… land or sea. His tour work had clearly arisen from his love of his land.

Con had been so quiet during our drive into the town of Dingle.

Then time stopped.

When time began again, Con was standing knee high in the Irish bay, holding a rope leading to a *curragh*, a handmade Irish boat made of canvas. The image of him standing there, holding the rope to the curragh, remains a permanent snap shot in my mind to this day. Except for his wet trousers, he was as well ironed and clean clothed as only an Irish mother can teach her son to be. I stayed quiet, not wanting to distract him from the depth of emotion he was clearly seeking to contain. Instead I watched the sky as clouds replaced the morning fog.

"Who are you?" Con suddenly shouted at me. He pressed his fists hard into his hipbones, trying to slow down the uninvited shaking that was taking over his tall, lean, outdoor body.

He dropped his head to his chest, overcome by what, I did not know. I only knew it bothered him greatly. He was looking out at the bay boats, loaded with ropes and fishing gear. The bay was calm. The fog that had caressed the dark cavernous waters had faded into the sunlight.

The question *'who are you?'* hung in the air.

When Con looked over at me, I noticed that his eyes were misty. Con was beautiful. Not in an effeminate or dandy kind of way. He radiated the vibrant spirit of a man whose soul stayed in sync with the sea. His heart beat the rhythm of the land. He had a fabulous ruddy complexion and wild red hair, clearly an offspring of buried Viking DNA resurfacing after many generations.

His hair blew with the wind and whipped across his face as he strode out of the bay, wet pants and all, and announced, *"I want to take you somewhere."*

At that time, I bordered the scales at around three hundred pounds. But as he grabbed my elbow, I felt myself lift out of my size into the svelte grace of a goddess.

We set out together in his jeep, which was well worn but still spiffy, neat and clean in true Irish fashion. As we passed road signs, I asked him what the words were underneath the main words, like 'Slea Head Drive'. He read the sign to me, first in Gaelic, and then in English. He explained, obviously offended, that the British did not bother to learn the Irish spelling and simply spelled their version of the names of the towns and roads phonetically, according to how they heard the words. Sometimes, when it was too difficult, they created entirely new names for places.

When I asked him about his connection to the language, he spoke with passion. He had grown up in a largely English-speaking home, but his father's love of the Gaelic language, along with the powerful Gaelic place names accorded to the wild landscape of his youth by his ancestors, resonated powerfully with him. He fell in love with the language at a young age.

In his early twenties, he suffered a life-changing climbing accident in Nepal. When he moved to the western tip of the Dingle Peninsula (Corca Dhibhne – place of the goddess, Dovina), he began to fully immerse himself in his original language and was now bi-lingual in English and Gaelic.

"And now, I have met you," he stated, looking at me sideways as he maneuvered the windy roads.

Con turned the jeep off the main road, and we headed straight up the side of a mountain.

As he drove, he slid through the last rain's mud, tires spinning out of control as he cantilevered us over jutting rocks using air as his roadway! No seat belt! Periodically, between squeezing my eyes shut and the force of hitting the next rut or rock jerking my eyes open, I saw greater and greater views of the surrounding landscape. It was a wonderland of blues, greens, grays, browns, and whites. The colors folded into each other, the stark gray, sheer cliffs topped by moss green meadows that coasted down into gray, over the sandy beaches. The beaches shrank in proportion to the increasing view of the enormity of the rich blue ocean, reflecting a tapestry of continuously changing clouds in a bright blue sky.

Reaching the top, Con agilely leapt from the jeep, no longer shaky, fully back on his own turf. He grabbed my hand and helped me, now completely shaken, out onto the rain soaked ground. *"Look…"* he whispered so quietly I almost missed what he said.

Following his gaze, I gasped at the panoramic view of all of western Ireland on one side and the unending Atlantic Ocean on the other. We were standing on the summit of Mount Eagle (Sliabh an Iolair) at the western end of the Dingle Peninsula.

I knew he had known to bring me here, where I could bask in the woven soul of earth and heaven. I finally turned, after a long, rich pause, the longest pause I had been in for many centuries, and looked into his eyes.

Con stared at me, *"Who are you? I remember you."*

I cannot write here the words he said to me that day, for that is between us and our souls. But he remembered. He remembered the awakened ways of the goddesses and the gods. He remembered the males of ancient times that guarded those goddesses and their people. He saw through the veil of the ordinary into the intimacy of otherworldliness.

He belonged to that intimacy of other worlds in other times where the voices of the forces had not been silenced. He belonged where the hands of the elemental natures of life caressed our faces with wind, sun, and rain. He belonged where the sea taught harsh lessons, where the dolphins sang with the villagers, and the goddesses brought the nurturing power of love to their people and their land.

He remembered me. I remembered him. We belonged.

"Your beloved and your friends were once strangers. Some-how at a particular time, they came from the distance toward your life. Their arrival seemed so accidental and contingent. Now your life is unimaginable without them. Similarly, your identity and vision are composed of a certain constellation of ideas and feelings that surfaced from the depths of the distance within you. To lose these now would be to lose yourself."

'Anam Cara: A Book of Celtic Wisdom'
—John O'Donohue

CHAPTER TWENTY-ONE

The Culture of Our Existence

Modern cultures took a long time to get here. The culture of our original existence stretches back to the beginning of life on this planet. All present cultures still carry the buried roots of that beginning. Those deep conscious connections to the earth bionetwork receded in the human mind long ago, leaving in their place only a shallow reminder of what lies waiting below the surface of human awareness. It does not matter that we have forgotten. Shadows of those memories continue to surface and return us to a deep powerful consciousness that pulses in every molecule of this planet and in us.

Con and I came from two very different cultures.

I was raised 'southern aristocrat', complete with a débutante ball and knowledge of how to set a proper table. Yet, something deep within me I could not put into words, had me rebel against the culture I was being raised in. There was a disconnect…everything seemed based on values that made no sense to me.

Iva, my best girlfriend, lived behind me in what was referred to as the 'wrong side of town', even though it bordered my back fence. I kept our friendship secret, scared that if found out I would be ostracized in some deeply disturbing way. Even back then, I knew something was terribly wrong and that something 'had' me that went way beyond the street I lived on.

I was not easy to raise. My life angered me and I yet adored my dad and deeply loved my mother. What ever bothered me went beyond the dilemma of my mother's drinking and my dad's long hours at the office. Something within me knew not to get stuck in my family dynamics. Something had messed with all of us. What, I did not yet know.

I was trained to dress up for Sundays, dresses only. I set the Sunday table each week, with the full array of multiple forks, knives, and spoons, even if we were only having hamburgers.

Anguish burned me.

Our backyard was well groomed by my grownup friend and handyman, a 'colored' man named Frank, from the 'colored' side of town. Frank kept my secrets. He planted around a place I had scooped out in my mother's flower garden so no one could see it. I would retreat during the day and sometimes at night and lie down in the dented earth, wrapped in an Indian blanket. I would curl up and listen to the sounds of the earth and the wordless communications I felt and knew with the wind and creatures, and to the voices caught in the walls of my 'more than proper side of town' house.

My 'right side of town' friends were lovely, yet I always felt out of place. I think we all did really. I think we all felt caught, not able to say what was in our hearts…conditioned to talk about, *"What kind of car does he drive?"*, or *"What does his father do?"*, or *"Oh!! (titter, titter, titter) look at what he gave me!"* or *"Let's go shopping!"* This constituted our reality.

One day, as I looked around the bed as we were laughing and tattling, I knew our future, which consisted of finding a husband and having children, had already left us barren and alone.

Something was missing.

A turning point in my rebellion was my coming out party, my débutante ball. Originally, this occasion meant the young woman was eligible to marry, and part of the purpose was to display her to eligible bachelors and their families with a view to marriage within a select upper class circle. To be a débutante, I had to be recommended by a distinguished committee or sponsored by an established member of elite society.

I was the youngest member of the Daughters of the American Revolution at that time and my mother was a member of the local elite society club. I was glad I lived in Tennessee. It horrified me that if I had lived further south I would have been referred to as a 'southern belle'.

Up until the moment of the 'ball', I kept my rebellion secret. That night I left the illusory culture of my upbringing and entered the culture of my 'true belonging'. I didn't know it at the time but my actions that night and the many to follow would eventually lead me to my own values and my own unique culture...myself.

My date for my débutante ball was my best friend Chick. I was presented in my gorgeous white chiffon gown, styled to look like a Greek Goddess. After the opening dance that presented me to society, we decided to leave. Before leaving, we snuck around and loaded our car with the sitting Buddhas that garnished the fake formal gardens in the country club ballroom. Though I am embarrassed about what I put my parents through, that prank still makes me smile. Little did I know that snatching those Buddhas was a premonition of things to come.

Con was raised across the sea in a culture with its own deeply rooted family and community ideals. The Catholic Church had a strong presence in Irish culture....family, community, and God.

Yet, we both carried a resonance with the earth and the netherworlds. We both found those connections more enticing than the social environments we came from.

We both had been initiated into the realms that lay hidden from view, lying in wait to rise to meet the ones who remembered.

Early on in our discussions of the trip, I realized I could go anywhere with Con. He not only could get me there, he would keep me safe. He was intensely aware of everything going on around him. He was proficient in the language of earth, sea, wind, fire, and rain. He innately knew people – how to have them move beyond what they thought they were capable of without even noticing he had moved them. He loved his land and had learned her stories and her people. When you listened to Con, you met the best of Ireland.

At that time, he had not yet met a 'me'.

I did not have the survival language of the earth, sea, wind, fire, and rain. I linked into the culture of existence that webbed together human beings and the Mother planet that loved them. I 'listened' to a meta-language of existence birthed in stillness that laced through the earth, sea, wind, fire, and rain and was once the original human language. I moved in that language until a transcendent state of connection was restored.

In that restoration, human beings remembered the true miraculous beings they were designed to be. I was designed to quest with the people and The Mother in that unifying point, that metapoint, that is the true connection between human beings and their planet, until that unifying point was awakened and enlivened them and they remembered.

Con and I began to learn each others 'listening' as we planned the trip. I was coming to his land and his way of 'listening'. We would find out what it was like to include what I was 'listening to'.

"Your mysteries lay hidden in stones that can't speak,
Thru' time all your wondrous knowledge we seek,
Be ye tomb or a temple we'd like to know why
On mid-winter's morning you seek light from the sky,
Your white quartz stones must have brightened the days
When the sun it shone down and reflected it's rays,
You refuse us a key or some Rosetta Stone,
We gaze on just Circles and Motifs and Bone."

'Newgrange' lyrics
—Wolfe Tones

chapter twenty-two

Newgrange

Con and I left the next morning for the trip from the western shore of Dingle to the eastern coast of Dublin. We picked up Adam on the way and headed for the airport. Adam and I would wait for the multiple flights that would bring in the thirty participants of the first quest. Con would go back to town to finish the last minute details of the trip. Adam had never seen much of his own country. I was as excited about the quest ahead for him as I was for the newbies we were picking up.

The day went easily. People came staggering off the plane giddy from both excitement and jet lag. The key to the success of the trip was to get them through jet lag as fast as possible, so we arranged for a hotel across from the airport where they could go straight to sleep upon arrival.

As we met everyone, I could tell how tired they were because they hardly even noticed Adam or me. But it was good to see them and to send them off for their naps. We left until the evening, when we would pick them up for a good Irish dinner and then return them to their hotel so they were awake enough to begin their adventure the next morning.

Con had come for dinner to meet everyone, and then he and Adam headed back to town for final supplies. I fell asleep 'listening'. Starting the next morning, we would enter 'the great mystery', only a mystery because we had forgotten. I fell asleep, excited to watch them as they 'remembered'.

Con thought we were heading straight for our first stop, Newgrange, a prehistoric megalithic passage tomb as old as the pyramids, dating back to around 3100 B.C. With everyone on board, I looked at Con and stated, *"I need to go to the sea."* His head almost hit the top of the minibus, he was so tall. He just looked at me. Grumbling under his breath, he drove us down a thin lane to the water. I got out of the bus and while people milled around I walked to the shore. I began a ritual that I would repeat every time I brought people to Ireland. I went to the edge of the waters, whether the ocean or one of thousands of inlets around the island fingers of the west coast and I said, *"Mother, I have brought you the children."*

This was my agreement with The Mother. I brought her 'her children' and every day took them to where she directed me.

The timing was perfect. When I turned to leave, everyone had been rounded up and put back on the bus.

We headed inland to Newgrange. Newgrange had been one of the places, like Glendalough, where I had managed to embarrass myself thoroughly. On one of my earlier trips to Ireland, I had been invited to come to the monument early one morning, before it was open for tourist trade. Now in the 2000's, there is an elaborate tourist centre where you take a small bus to the site and then return by bus to the centre.

Not when I went. Then, the taxi man drove up a small road, parked on the side, went to a large shed that took payment in pounds, and then passed through the gate of a small, dark, painted picket fence. The morning I visited, the air was very clear. As I got out of the car, I could see down the Boyne Valley and for a second, thought I saw faint outlines of men, women and children approaching Newgrange.

Since I was an invited guest, I did not have to pay. The female guide let me through the gate and as we walked toward the tomb, she shared all the lore and the facts associated with it. The outlines of the men, women and children coming up toward the tomb were becoming more distinct. I felt a knot in my belly, and a longing that seemed to be stimulated by the vision out of the corner of my eye.

Nervous, I asked the lovely guide if I could just sit down on the ground a minute. Delighted I was being affected by the place, she guided me to a wooden guide marker jutting out of the ground where I could lean, taking the pressure off my back.

The world around me disappeared. Open eyed, I stared at the scene before me. Men and women were carrying objects wrapped in coarse cloth. Whatever was wrapped up stuck out in all directions like a badly wrapped package. As they crossed into the grounds in front of the tomb, I realized that the packages contained bones, large bones. Each package carried a skull and skeleton broken up to make them easy to carry.

The women and men went into the tomb, which was covered with ornate carvings. A long oblong stone seemed to block the front of the entrance. On it were deeply grooved spirals and wavy lines that looked like ocean waves. Out of body now, I followed them. The light was coming through a boxed window over the entrance. It pierced the dark over our heads, shining in front of us until we got to the back of the tomb.

The tomb had a three-leaf clover configuration at the back. Each leaf of the clover contained a small chamber with carvings on the walls. The men and women placed each package onto a flat much used circular stone and opened it. Leaving the bones and skulls exposed, they added moist grass, small dry twigs and tucked small cloth-wrapped packages around the bones.

Once this was done, a druid priest and priestess came into the enclosure with embers. Swinging the embers in slingshot looking carriers, each of them went ceremoniously to each chamber. Using these embers, they lit the wrappings, starting a small fire. They sat in each chamber after the men and women of the village had filed out, speaking words that elicited a powerful energy field. After a while they came out to the villagers, who stood waiting.

The Druid priests and priestesses walked toward the young children. I could hear the hopeful cry of the parents as they neared a child and a sigh of disappointment if they passed by. There were about thirty people there, and of those thirty, maybe seven or eight children. Finally the Druids chose three children. The parents were hugging and kissing them with tears of joy. Then each child followed the Druids into the tomb and sat cross-legged in front of the burning bones.

I realized what was happening. In the ceremony, the bones of deceased Druid priests were being burned and the children in front of them had been chosen to carry on their legacy. Time passed as I watched and as the children came out, each child received a long robe and bulky leggings from the druids. As two of the priests, still quiet and regal, left with the children, the vision faded into the villagers' daily life.

Men and women worked side by side, the women strong like the men. Some women and men worked together binding leather straps, for what, I did not know. Younger men and women tilled the ground while children ran around playing.

I was no longer around the tomb, but down the valley by the river, now called The Boyne. The experience of this small community was one of trust, co-operation, and love. The depth of community and mutuality of existence awakened an ancient longing in me. It also awakened a memory of the way people once lived together, how they worked in sync.

I watched as they finished their work in a harmonic symphony, a day well done, and then faded into an evening of food and song. The vision went on for a long time. I was transfixed by the common sharing of life, no hierarchy, only fraternity. With that memory and experience of equality, shared work, and reverence for life, my heart shattered and I wept for the loss of it in our modern worlds.

I mean I wept. I was so bitterly overcome with loss they had to move me out of the way so I wouldn't disturb the visitors who were arriving to see the tomb. They even had my taxi driver stay with me, I was so distraught. I was oblivious to the world around me. I was in the presence of how community was designed to be in its purest form. Waves and waves of memory shattered everything I had put up with. I knew that I needed, not wanted, but needed to find that kind of community in this lifetime. My future destiny was set in place.

Now I had brought thirty people to Newgrange. I could still comb my eyes over the grounds, remembering what I had remembered before, even though the overwhelming impact had dulled. Starting our journey with the more 'on the tourist track' places had been a wise decision. The trip had started well. After Newgrange, we would head for Tara, and then spend the rest of the day traveling to Killarney.

"Éist fuaim ! An Chláirseach !
Ar bharr Teamhair
Seo chugaibh an tArd ri
Ar bharr Teamhair
Listen to the sound of the harp!
The High Kings have arrived on the Hill of Tara"

Song: 'Tara'
Album: 'Two Horizons'
—Moya Brennan

ChAPTER TWENTY-ThREE

The Hill of Tara

I warned Con when we were planning our trip, that we could not follow any hour-by-hour trip plan. Little did he realize!

Leaving Newgrange, we headed for the hills of Tara. Michael, another guide, brought up Con's jeep and took over the minibus.

One of the participants on the trip, Marilyn, was an innocent and lively woman who could have been an art teacher in a school for deprived children. She brought such beauty to the world. Her pale white skin, pixie haircut and twinkling way of speaking made her seem elfin-like.

Over the years I had known her, I was aware how easy it was for her to 'connect in'. She was profoundly moved by the different realms that played with her and she shared them effusively. She worked for a company that bought and sold replacement parts for the human body. I thought she had that job so that the replacement parts carried her extra spark of life for the humans who needed them.

Tara was the seat of the High Kings of Ireland, a place of great power. Even though nothing but mounds now existed on the surface, the pulse of ancient ways poured through the historic site, creating a quiet that is to this day unmarred. We introduced the participants to wandering, especially after being in the 'controlled guide' through Newgrange. Every step was designed for a slow calculated descent into the depth of ourselves and what waited for us there.

As the time approached for us to resume our cross country trip to the Gap of Dunloe, our next stop, I noticed Marilyn lying spread-eagle across a mound belly up, eyes squeezed shut, smiling so hard I thought she was going to disappear into it. Michael, our new driver, had rounded up everyone and gotten them on the bus.

I realized that Marilyn was in a 'hit'. That is my name for it. When the consciousness of the planet opens its arms again to her children, something happens. Mostly what happens is a stillness that is so compelling, the person simply cannot move. They could be sitting on the ground and find themselves sinking into the ground and not able to get up. They might start crying, and once they can move, need to touch every tree and blade of grass. When someone experiences a 'hit', a reconnection to the juice of life reclaims them.

I ran over and told Michael we couldn't go yet, that Marilyn was in a 'hit'.

Michael explained, in strained tolerance, that we were going to be late to our next stop. I explained again that Marilyn was in a 'hit'.

"What's a 'hit'?" he mumbled. I explained which made things worse.

"Jeez!"

When I refused to go, he stormed over to Con, colorfully exasperated about our delay. In a very loud voice that boomed over the winds that whip through the mounds of Tara and looking straight at me, Con announced to Michael, *"There is regular time, there is Irish time, and NOW there is Tantra time!!!"*

After about a half hour, Marilyn wobbled over with Con's help to the bus. She snuggled into a seat in the back, radiant and smiling, with small tears leaking slowly out of her eyes.

We drove on to our next appointment with the land.

Interestingly enough, we always got everything done in the day. Time moves with the land into the wonder of 'no time'. Time adjusted itself quite conveniently, so that none of us would miss out on the moments of connection that were so essential to the vitality and grace of the human spirit.

This wouldn't be the only time I taxed the very generous Irish spirit of Con and Michael. I would announce that we had to go here or there, often taking us totally off the charted course.

Con once as frustrated as Michael asked, *"Why?"*

"Listen," I responded.

"By Killarney's lakes and fells,
Em'rald isles and winding bays;
Mountain paths and woodland dells,
Mem'ry ever fondly strays.
Bounteous nature loves all lands
Beauty wonders ev'rywhere;
Footprints leaves on many strand,
But her home is surely there!
Angels fold their wings and rest,
In that Eden of the west
Beauty's home Killarney,
Heaven's reflex Killarney."

—*Irish Folksong*

CHAPTER TWENTY-FOUR

Killarney

We would arrive in the afternoon in Killarney and spend the night so people could rest and prepare for camping the next few nights. I figured getting them as close to the land as possible, as fast as possible, was the best way to put them squarely in the grip of The Mother.

As we stopped for photos and short views on our way, participants began to ask me what the agenda was and were often startled to hear that there were not a lot of activities crammed into each day. Slowing the rapid pace of Americans so they could fall into their depth was a challenge I knew was going to occur, because I had directly experienced Ireland slowing me down. Con was far more gracious about my timeline. After years of taking Americans on trips, Con had developed a certain balance between what he knew to do and what pleased the new kids on the block from North America.

My friend David was going to meet me in Killarney. What an unexpected surprise! I asked Adam if he wanted to go, and a young woman named Tasha. I had wanted David and Tasha to meet for some time so I was thrilled that this coincidence had occurred.

While the rest of the participants were settling into their B&B's, we met David and went for tea just outside of Killarney in a tiny village. Tea was at a minuscule shop at the end of a long line of row houses, squeezed in between the road and the edge of a bridge canvassed in sizable boulders.

Tasha and I made our way down to the small gurgling stream that flowed under the bridge. We sat on the boulders that lined the stream while the boys went to get us tea. The stream was just large enough for two swans that floated in a blue algae green pool in the center of it.

I will never forget the image of the two lanky-legged young men walking out of the shop. My friend David was ten years younger than I was and nine years older than Adam. Adam balanced a tray with dainty Victorian teacups and a Victorian 'pot of tea' covered with a covey to keep it warm. David carried another tray with an assortment of biscuits on an equally dainty Victorian plate. As they were navigating the stones down to where we were, the swans came waddling out of the stream making a beeline for the biscuits.

I shouted at Adam, who was obstructing the swan's trek to the biscuits, just as the swan shot out its head and neck ready to take a bite of him. Adam jumped up in the air, pirouetting, trying to avoid the swan and keep the tea tray balanced at the same time.

The other swan slipped past him and headed straight for my friend. David swung right and left trying to keep from getting bitten by the loudly honking swan that was clear the biscuits were for him. The scene of David dodging the persistent honking swan and Adam leaping in the air to avoid being bitten was hysterical.

Tasha and I exploded into fits of laughter, which didn't help matters. It just looked so funny, two semi-grown men dancing around two swans, trying to not drop the trays. It reminded me of gunslingers firing at the feet of men to make them dance. The swans were actively after the boys, and the boys were actively avoiding the swans. Suddenly, the trays flipped up into the air in unison, teacups and biscuits flying in all directions. The tea covey slipped off the teapot as it shot up into the air, turned over, spilled its tea and came crashing down on the rocks, in a 'grand finale'.

Victorious, the two swans carefully picked through the broken dish to get to the biscuits, devouring them, and then honking and chatting away as they made their way back to the stream.

The two men, clearly upset, neither used to humble pie, went back into the shop to explain what had happened. Leaving behind any desire for tea, David decided he would treat us to a fine dinner at the most expensive five star hotel in all of Ireland.

An elegant meal was a great indulgence! This was one of those times when I was grateful that my mother trained me in manners and formal dining. I knew what all the forks, spoons and knives were for and actually enjoyed the elegance of luxurious living occasionally.

After we finished the meal, it was obvious that David and Tasha were interested in spending the night together. As he paid for the dinner he said, *"Why don't I get us some rooms! My treat! Wouldn't you rather stay here than in the B&B?"*

I asked David if he would take Adam back to where everyone else was. He agreed. The day's activities were over anyway, and all that remained was to go back and retire to my room, so I said yes!

I was amazed at my hotel room. I have stayed in gorgeous quarters in my lifetime, but this was a first. The room was Victorian style, with heavy velvet drapes that fell from a 14-foot ceiling and covered double doors that led out to my own private garden. In true British style, the garden was closed in back, with six-foot bushes carefully trimmed to look like one long bush. A walkway wound through the multi-colored flower beds, buzzing with bees, even though it was late at night.

A small round black ornate wrought-iron table enhanced the center of the garden with two matching chairs. A cabana covered the dining area. The young man who escorted me to my room explained that breakfast would be served in the private garden. In the morning, at whatever time I chose, the hotel would leave a cart under the cabana.

He then asked me if I wanted him to turn down the bed and draw my bath. There was only to say yes! With no break in his gracious demeanor, he left the room for a moment and came back with a robe large enough for me. Before he drew my bath, he asked if I would like a lavender or rose-scented bath.

I was the queen in her kingdom being cared for by her faithful servant. He retreated to the bath, letting me know he would be about fifteen minutes so that I could change into my robe. He urged me to get in right away after the bath was drawn. Realizing that no one could see me, I undressed, threw back the curtains and opened the doors to let in the cool night air. As I breathed in, letting the fresh air relax me, I felt beautiful.

After he drew the bath, he quietly left the room, letting me know I did not need to tip him. Everything had been taken care of. The bathroom continued the Victorian splendor with an old-fashioned bathtub on lion claw feet. The bathroom had every possible amenity. An elegant tray at the foot of the bathtub overflowed with of a variety of soaps, shampoos and conditioners. Huge beach-sized towels were folded under a wrought-iron towel rack. The stained glass window depicted a floral garden. He had lit candles encased in glass that created a dance of reflection as I turned off the lights and slipped into the bath.

Beside the tub was a bowl of rose petals. I threw some of them into the bath, laid back against the perfect slope of the tub and promptly fell asleep.

I vaguely heard the door into my bedroom open and close but didn't think very much about it, thinking the valet had brought another unimaginable, delicious treat for me. I stepped out of the tub, dried off with the thick luscious towel, wrapped the towel around me and went into the main room.

Adam was curled up on the bed.

"Your friend told me he thought we were an item. I told him I thought so too."

Nothing could be more shocking or erotic than a gorgeous man, naked from the waist up, leaning on a plush dark maroon pillow, covered by the most elaborately woven damask bedspread in greens and purples, smiling and speaking with a lilting Irish accent.

I just stood there. He slipped off the bed and walked over to me. Taking my free hand, the one that wasn't gripping the towel, he walked me to the other side of the huge bed. He kissed me on the nose, and with one soft and sensuous move, pulled the towel off of me. I just stood there.

This wasn't happening. I had the distinct feeling I was watching a movie and that I couldn't possibly be part of it. The bed was still turned down on my side. I don't know how he did it, but he guided me under the covers, tucked them in around me, went around to his side of the bed and curled in.

He pulled me over to him, my head resting on his strong shoulder. Somehow, between tucking me in and curling into bed, he had removed his shorts. Naked felt right. I remember thinking that. He shifted until I was firmly enclosed against his side. He kissed me on the nose again and quietly slipped into sleep. I felt myself follow him.

Deep in the night, I was not sure if I was dreaming or awake. I was in a state of euphoria. The world felt supernatural. I was not a body. I was a tenuous form, shape-shifting in one essence of experience after another, molding and shaping to the nebulous form beside me. Quintessence, the purest essence, the fifth element, and the most perfect embodiment of what we really are, neutralizing the force of gravity, opened up the doorway of passion from a place that I had never before experienced. As I was moved and shaped both within and without by forces that create the fundamentals of life, I wondered if he was oblivious to it, sleeping away beside me, with me now cradled fully in his arms.

I woke. Everything was so quiet. The air quivered with anticipation. The room glowed with a transparency of energy that made the bed seem as if it were suspended in an energy field separate from the rest of the room. I felt shaken by what I was experiencing. The experience felt shared, which scared me most of all.

"Are you awake?" Adam asked softly.

"Yes," I whispered.

"Grand," he murmured as he shifted to take me all the way in.

"Black Valley
Leaping through the heather wild
Where the sly red fox prowls
In the starlit midnight air
To grab a timid lamb in Croc
While Purple Mountain and Reeks just stare"

—Poem written by pupils of the
Black Valley National School

CHAPTER TWENTY-FIVE

The Black Valley

Up until now, I had been alone or with someone Irish when I was walking the land, being disturbed and awakened by its spirits. So I was completely unprepared for the effect it had on these seemingly stable women who had come on this first trip with me. I was aware of the pretense that we Americans lived in, and how hard it was for people to relax. This was perturbing, for these were the people I thought *were* relaxed. I was glad I did not have an uptight businessman on the trip if these savvy ladies were having trouble calming down.

I had invited them to the land of silence. I knew the stillness, the lack of airplanes flying overhead, the void of the noise of major highways, left an emptiness that could only be filled by depth. I also knew Ireland did not have the amenities that we had in the United States in the 1990's. For instance, there were no washers or dryers easily at hand.

I had asked them to pack hardy clothes they could wear over and over again and to pack light. Clearly they had not gotten the message. Almost everyone brought a gigantic suitcase or two as well as nice outfits. Thank goodness they had, however, brought the full top and bottom raingear and most of them had brought sturdy shoes. For those who didn't, Con and Michael had stopped in Killarney to purchase them. Con was invaluable as he guided each person to get exactly what they needed.

I noticed that during our trip down, there was so much talking. I hadn't realized how used to the silence I had gotten until I was on the bus with the 'crowd'. We had been to Tara and marveled at Newgrange, the more tourist-oriented aspects of the trip.

"Break them in gently", I thought. I had learned from my solo trips to Ireland that there are forces here that want us to remember, want us to be without fear, and want us to be hardy in ourselves. So I knew to bring the people to the land and then listen to where they were to go. I never would hold it as *my* trip. I was asked to *'bring the stones home'*. I was not told what to do with them. I was only asked to bring them to the land. The land, the elementals, and the forces would take care of everything else.

On the way down, a chocolate obsession had begun. I must say, there was a really good case to make for Irish chocolate. I had no idea how much paraffin there was in chocolate made in the USA. In Ireland, the chocolate is so rich; the phrase 'mouth watering' has real truth. The already existing agitation of not knowing how to be in the background of silence, coupled with the sudden overwhelming need for chocolate, had now created a cackle of voices on a sugar high, rising in increasing volume.

Being in an even deeper silence given the night before, when the three of us joined the rest of the participants on the bus, I thought I was stranded in a chicken coop!

Everyone was dressed 'somewhat' for the great outdoors. Off we headed to The Gap of Dunloe, *Bearna an Choimín* in Irish, and the Black Valley. The Black Valley is a remote location in the Macgillycuddy's Reeks that lies beyond the Gap of Dunloe, nestled against Moll's Gap. The valley is part of the Kerry Way, a walker's version of the Ring of Kerry, beginning and ending in Killarney. The valley was not connected to telephone networks or to electricity at the time we were there.

I had decided to bring people over the pass at the Gap of Dunloe into the Valley, while Con, the other guides and our chef set up camp. It was great to have the group at Kate Kearney's Cottage at the mouth of the Gap. Watching people be in the presence of the congeniality of the Irish was wonderful to behold.

I was thrilled. Here the participants would discover the power of the Irish spirit in the people themselves. Leaving the pub, we headed next to where the Poneymen had their 'traps' for hire. The men all lived in and around the Gap, as did their families and ancestors. The Poneymen use a system called 'The Turn', which determines who takes the next passengers. 'The Turn' has been going on since the 1920's and has been passed down from one generation to the next.

There is an intensity that happens when people have been together a long time. When they have been friends and family for many years, and you are invited into their haven, you become an instant friend. It isn't put on. It is real. In Ireland, you get a real taste of the foundational spirit of the land. You are the beloved. You are joked with, entertained, and beguiled by the nature of the land that expresses itself in the twinkle of their eyes and their remarkable talent for storytelling.

Each Poneyman has his own stories woven into the history of the Gap.

The horse-drawn traps I had hired, readied to take us on an excursion up and down the pass. Everyone piled in. Two to four participants sat facing each other. The Gap Poneyman stood at the front. Impressively sized horses shook their manes as the Irishmen picked up the reins. One by one the traps left, the Poneymen guiding the horses up the Gap. That is not all they did. The men would entertain their overseas passengers with lore while the passengers sat enthralled by the unique Gap of Dunloe dialect.

I stopped for a minute to greet the man in whose trap I always rode. He had a fiddle and I loved riding with him. Every time he got to a gutted and abandoned stone inn, with only the remaining stone frame standing, he stopped, broke into song and played his fiddle. Those moments of him playing were one of the things I loved to repeat again and again.

This day, he pulled the cart up in front of the abandoned primitive inn, and tweed cap a bit askew, a bit of pint in his belly, stood in the center of the small cart that squeezed four people. His horse didn't move an inch as he played --the twang of the breezy notes elicited both a need to dance and a deep melancholy. It floated through the air, heightening the sensation of pleasure not only for this moment, but for all of life. After he finished playing, he told them just as he had me, about how his father had played for the people who once came and stayed at the now lonely, empty inn.

Mesmerized, the four newbies continued their jostling ride up the narrow stone road in the constant conundrum of whether to look at the picturesque Gap or the face of the Poneyman. A wonderful dilemma!

I had talked Adam into taking a horse up the Gap with me. I didn't realize that what they might call a horse, we would term a pony. Adam's legs were so long, they hung loose, almost dragging along the ground... and he had the tallest horse available. Going up to the top of the Gap was no problem, but when we started back down the other side, I realized that if you have never ridden before, a horse clattering at a gallop down a steep narrow road built of stone could be a challenge.

Out in front of me, Adam's horse had his full head. Adam didn't seem to realize that he could pull back on the reins.

All I could see were his long, lanky legs flapping up and down as he held on tight and his lively animal charged home.

I tried not to laugh when I caught up with him. However, the Irish Poneymen held no such reserve. I knew the story of Adam flapping down the Gap on one of their horses would enter the local lore for generations to come.

After our trip up and down the Gap, we loaded into vans and headed back over the pass for the Black Valley. I would have thought the waterfalls springing out of Macgillycuddy's Reeks and the landscape of early spring flowers would have silenced even the most hardcore tourist. But no, the giddy drunkenness of the land persisted, and the chatter got louder and louder. I realized that the chatter was the result of the intense, pure energy of the land and its myriad connections. The nonstop talking was bothering neither the land nor the Irish. But I was incredibly clear that the ceaseless chatter was indeed bothering me.

I had not realized how deep I had come within myself. The surface talk, which at some level had always been alien to me, now was intolerable. The land and its mysteries had whipped me into silence. I treasured the silence that happened in reverent connection with this land.

We arrived in Black Valley near dusk. The tents were all up. The chef had begun preparing our meal in the largest tent. Most of the people had never camped. So the agitation and discomfort of no electricity, no telephones, and the dark on its way, pretty much put them over the edge. We were camped in a flat area between the mountains. Sheep roamed nearby and the silence hung over the landscape, palpable and thick. From the group, a multi-voiced babble rose to fill the silence. They hovered together prattling away like hens in a henhouse.

I broke, furious, and bellowed at them in a fierce, snarling voice, *"I swear to God, if you don't stop talking I will strike you with lightning!"*

In the next second, wind filled the valley. The clouds above us darkened and a huge bolt of lightning burst out of the sky, striking the hillside on our left. A deafening clap of thunder smacked the air, the sky opened up, and a pounding rain slammed the ground with such force, all the tents flattened.

I stood in shock as the participants fled for the chef's tent, the only one left standing. I let the rain drench me as I watched everyone huddle together trying to stay dry. I had gotten my silence. Wide-eyed and drenched, they weren't saying a word.

Camping in the Black Valley had become a disaster. Con had torn the oil pan out on his brand new jeep while bringing in the tents and he and the guides had left to get another vehicle. The chef was stoned, so I had no idea what kind of meal we were going to end up with or even if we were going to have a meal. The tents were soaked. Without Con and the guides and with the chef having a grand ole time, oblivious to the conditions around him, putting tents back up was relegated to the participants. Thank goodness the suitcases were still in the vehicles. They were saved from the drench.

The hammering rain stopped as suddenly as it had started.

Adam built a fire next to a stone wall that ran across the valley. The Irish build stone walls everywhere. Some of them were built to designate The Land. The Land was a section of ground that an Irishman had carved out for himself and his family. Intense clashes happened over disputed land. The Land was sacrosanct for the Irish ancestors. The rest of the usually four-foot stone walls were built simply to have a place to put the stone that had been dug out of the ground to make room to plant crops.

Around the beaches of Ireland, women would carry long, round baskets on their backs, secured by a cloth rope they tied round their forehead; the long basket hung from the back of their head down to their waist. They would walk with their men to the sea, gather seaweed, and then carry the seaweed up the steep slopes to The Land. Then they would spread the rocky ground with seaweed and pummel the remaining stone into powder to create the proper conditions to plant potatoes.

The Irish worked hard for every piece of soil they could bring to life in a land not well suited to providing. Later, the British would have the Irish build walls and roads that went nowhere, just to justify giving them a loaf of bread at the end of the day, bread made by the Irish from the grains grown on their own land.

The stone was placed with artistic precision. Each wall had its own design, the rocks chosen to fit perfectly so that it was strong and would last many generations. And last they did.

I went to bed. I had turned the Americans over to The Mother. I had lost my cool and I needed to open up some space to see what was going on. I fell asleep immediately. Adam woke me up in the pitch dark of the night around ten. I could hear people laughing and talking. He said, *"I think you better come out here. Some boys from town heard about us being here and have come out to have a pint with us,"* a pint being a measure of beer for the drinking.

I came out of the tent into an amazing scene. People had gathered stones to sit on. The fire Adam had started was roaring. There were three lads in their early twenties drinking and talking with the group. The chef was nowhere to be found. Con had not returned.

I realized what Adam was talking about. One of the lads was sitting, leaning against the wall, his feet almost in the fire, anesthetized by alcohol and tipping over dangerously close to the flames.

The other lads were sober enough. There is no drinking on the trip, yet sobriety is a dubious term in Ireland. There is a drunkenness that requires no alcohol. It is the drunkenness of a good time with good talk and great company. It was clear, that was what was going on here. In the meantime, I needed to make sure we didn't have a human bonfire that night.

I asked one of the lads to pull the intoxicated youth away from the fire. He walked over to the young man and whispered something into his ear. *"No foreigner is going to make me move off my land!"* he responded. *"You tell her to leave. This is my land!"*

Sean introduced himself to me and told me that Liam, the

inebriated lad, had just come home from the United States where he had been working for eleven years to support his mum and da, sisters and brothers. I felt for him. I grabbed Adam's hand, and we walked around the fire to the wall holding Liam somewhat up.

"I don't want to ever take you from your land," I whispered in his ear, *"I just don't want you to get burned up in the fire. Will you let Adam move you over a bit so you don't catch on fire?"*

Liam thought that was a good idea and was quite appreciative when he got our genuine concern. After Adam moved him and propped him up so he could remain upright, Liam asked if he could sing us a song. This was a great honor. Singing is one of their greatest gifts.

I told him we would be honored and he began to sing. He sang of a land he had had to leave, a land he loved, a land he had missed so much his heart ached to return. He sang so poignantly and powerfully, his voice carried over the crackling fire, filling the silence with the strife and courage of the Irish. He began to weep, yet his voice carried on. He began to sing of his return, the joy in his heart and how he wished to never be separated from his homeland again.

The other lads joined in as he switched into a song about a young Irish girl who was about to be married and about the landlord who came for his due. One of the many wicked acts of the English landlords was that if a maiden was to be married, they claimed the right to lie with her before her wedding night.

The firelight flickered on tear-stained cheeks. As the song

ended, the silence no longer needed to be enforced. The doorway had opened. The silence had entered. The magic of Ireland was upon us.

Everyone sat so still, they looked like living statues, contemplating the earth, the fire and the sky. One of the participants on our journey, Barbara, was a large African American woman. Working as a terminal care nurse, Barbara was born and raised in New Jersey and had never been out of the country until now. She had tended to the final hours of many prominent men and women whose families had been linked to the early fortunes of our country. At an early age, Barbara had met a spiritualist named May.

During the first consult I did with Barbara, not knowing about May, I saw a woman who had crossed over. She handed me a rose and asked me to be Barbara's spiritual guide. I found it uncomfortable to take the place of an intriguing spiritualist who had guided Barbara's unconquerable spirit from the time she was a teen. Yet, the power of what is *so* persists, and Barbara and I moved into the legacy that May had left us.

The older cultures of hospitality understand something shared from the heart must be shared in return by the heart of another. Barbara stood up. Her large, sweet bulk, silhouetted by the fire, evoked the presence of the Great Mother. She said, *"I would like to sing a song for you to thank you for sharing your land with us."* With that introduction, and in a stunning, deep, evangelical gospel voice, she belted out, *"Amazing Grace, how sweet the sound that saved a wretch like me...."*

The lads stood, propping up Liam between them. They knew they were in the presence of the Great Mother of their land. All of us less cultured scrambled to our feet. Once on our feet we could feel the earth was pulsing with love. The stars sparkled with appreciation. We reached for each other's hands. Thirty-three people stood around the fire, in unity with life, belting out the words of a song from a shared heart.

After the lads had gone and everyone was tucked in, Adam and I crawled into our tent to sleep in the deep, dark, night. I knew we had entered the webbing that existed here in this place of home for all.

You just never know when the portals are going to open. Sometimes, they open where you least expect it. Sometimes, they open when an Irish lad shows up at your campsite in the middle of nowhere, gets drunk with his lads, leans against his wall, and invites everyone in.

"The sun was sinking o'er the westward
The fleet is leaving Dingle shore
I watch the men row in their curraghs
as they mark the fishing grounds near Skellig Mor
All through the night men toil until the daybreak
while at home their wives and sweethearts kneel and pray
That God might guard them and protect them
And bring them safely back to Dingle Bay"

—*An Irish Ballad*

Chapter twenty-six

Dingle

The Irish don't give a hoot whether you are famous or gorgeous.

When a movie was filmed a few years before, an Irish farmer had a stand-in part to hold the rope of a mule along a strip of road. They told him to stay there until they came to get him.

A well known gorgeous actress had gotten lost and her car

had broken down. She saw the farmer and hiked quite a distance to get to him. When she got there, she asked the farmer if he could help her get to the nearest village to get a mechanic. The farmer kept replying, *"Said I'd watch this mule until they come and get me."* Finally, frustrated beyond control, the actress shouted, *"Don't you know who I am????*
I'm _____!" The farmer, not batting an eye replied, *"Good to meet you, _____. I'm Mr. McNally."*

I spent several evenings in a pub in Dublin listening to Van Morrison sing while he was hanging out there. I watched as U2 came in for a pint, and everyone greeted them with the same hospitality they greeted everyone else. This was true for both men and women. Pubs were places where older men came to drink all day, just like in the USA, but also where families came for soup and soda bread lunches. Boys and girls, men and women, gathered to chat. I learned the art of chatting in Ireland. Powerful storytellers!

The very way the Irish moved and spoke was inside story. There was a robust relationship to living, when every minute, every move was the marvel of an original self-expressed, full of life story…tragedy or comedy…no matter…full on!

That was how these young male guides, 'the boys' I affectionately came to call them, existed…full on! Under the light-hearted robust conversations and the full-on playfulness was an innate understanding that these stories fulfilled the treasure of time. I have to say there was a skill about it too.

On the trip from Dublin to Killarney, from Killarney to the Gap of Dunloe, then the Black Valley, story after story was being formed, now not only in the verve of 'the boys', also in the 'new dawn' eyes of the participants. In the new memory of the Black Valley, the sightseeing trip had ended. Telltale signs revealed that the extraordinary had interrupted the ordinary. What started as a trip had at last become the Vision Quest, a journey toward the recognition of the soul. The forces of life had permeated the sheath wrapped around the hearts and souls of these beautiful people, fulfilling an unknown need that reached to the roots of their existence.

None of the participants had ever been around such a bevy of men who were so full of vibrant life. I had spent the past several years trying to get used to the way the Irish look right at you, see you, laugh with you, and enjoy you. Yet my heart is still refreshed and delighted by these encounters. I went through my initiation. I was startled at first, when they put their arm around me to escort me through the door, then embarrassed when they looked deep into my eyes like a lover while telling their latest tale.

And then I finally relaxed, no longer self-conscious or awkward with it all. Now freed from all my past programming, I loved being enjoyed just because I was there. I had gratefully fallen into the same innate pleasure of being with another, simply for the sake of sharing space on this planet. I am so clear this is the way it is meant to be when seduction is not present…the grace of unity that the males and females of our species were designed to enjoy. Adam and Eve playing in the garden before seduction was a part of us.

'The boys' were part of recognizing our souls.

Sue, one of the participants, a well-known and well-respected therapist in her late forties, was totally hypnotized by one of the spunky early-thirties lads. The excitement of being with such attractive, vivacious men who enjoyed a woman of any age without an agenda was intoxicating.

As they were walking toward the bus, he carried the large tent she had shared with another woman, leaving her free from carrying anything. You could imagine a boy carrying a girl's books home from school and how good it would make the young girl feel, being cared for by a man. As Sue, wide-eyed and feasting on Aidan's every word, walked toward the bus, she slipped.

Without a break in conversation and without even apparently noticing, Aidan reached out his arm under hers, interrupted her fall, stabilized her, and continued their walk as if nothing had happened.

This is why I loved 'the boys'. They were there for us in every way. Yes, some of the women were definitely interested in some other ways that I had asked 'the boys' not to partake of, but pretty soon they all fell into line as human beings with other human beings, raw in the primal joy of living with nothing sexually explicit added.

The movement of the bus managed to periodically rock all of us to sleep as we headed over the winding roads to Dingle. The bus was quiet. Some people were writing in their journals. Others were staring glassy-eyed at nothing in particular. The profundity of the mystery had begun.

Con would meet us in Dingle, the small fishing village that

semi-circled the dark murky waters of Dingle Bay where I swam with Fungi just a few years before. Never dulled to the rolling hills, the jagged mountains, and moist lush valleys laced with streams, I still felt awe at the first initial impact of coming around the curvy road that led to Dingle from the east and seeing the sea and the bay stretched out before me.

Dingle bustled with life. Shops lined the half moon curve of the land, which faced fishing boats as far as the eye could see. 'Quaint' carried an entirely new meaning in the western part of Ireland. Though shops were lovely, painted in various colors, and the hustle and bustle of the normal life of a small busy town was everywhere, the throbbing hardiness of carving out a life began to press into the new visitors. A soon-to-be-common, 'uncommon discomfort' began to surface beneath the exterior of their delight at being there.

Having weathered our first camping expedition, Con had gone ahead to the Blaskets to set up our tents on the island. Now having connected powerfully to the land in The Black Valley, we would now connect to the sea that surrounded the three mile long Great Blasket Island. The depth of the ocean would restore the deeper intimacy of our own being. I knew that by being on the land and on the sea, the Earth Mother would do her job, absorbing her children back into her body, giving them back the safety of their home.

On this first trip, I had not realized that it might take supernatural means to have that connection happen. I discovered I was naive in what actually would 'bring the stones home'.

Ireland was a schoolroom of immense natural learning,

needing no help from me. Natural experience is natural learning. On these trips, I discovered some interesting sources of that learning when Americans, accustomed to the amenities of an affluent life visited Ireland. On the surface, Ireland looked affluent enough, but as they looked for coffee, a place to do their nails, or a laundromat, they were shaken, not realizing that those amenities concealed a foreboding that they wouldn't know how to be without normal comforts. This was the tricky part of the trip. Let the land and the people provide what is needed. I learned never to manipulate any experience. Just to let things be.

Con had arranged to have us camp on the Blaskets, not an easy thing to do. The Great Island had very little level ground. Con had been generous, though not particularly pleased in granting my wish.

Tomorrow we were going there. Today we would all put up in a local inn and rest, shop and be tourists for a bit, before continuing on our journey.

"Drawn together by forces beyond all measure
Human and creature or creature and creature
That is the mystery...."

'What Am I?'
—*Poem by Tantra Maat*

CHAPTER TWENTY-SEVEN

The Sea Lion and Her Pup

Shortly past dawn, with the haze of fog misting every-thing, we straggled out of our beds to drive to the Blaskets ferry. Everyone had loved being in a region of Ireland that was 'Gaeltacht', Gaelic speaking. The wealth of the Irish experience was sinking in.

Out from Dingle, we wound around Slea Head Drive. The road follows the coastline with a sheer drop on the left. As the morning cleared, we saw the beehive shaped stone homes of an early people, up on the hill to the right. As the cliff drew closer to the road, a stone wall was built to protect travelers but not block the view. We stopped at the farthest point of Slea Head, where it jutted out into the sea and where the road turns to meander toward the ferry opposite the Blaskets. The Great Island was the only one open for tourists.

At our turning point, there was a grotto opposite the cliff walls overlooking the sea. A weathered statue of Christ with Mary Magdalene and Mother Mary kneeling before him, all painted white, stood in front of a lone high hill. Up close, on the figure of Jesus, a flow of rust-colored paint signified blood coming from his hands and his feet.

We took a break to breathe the fresh air, enjoy the view and avoid the possible auto nausea that came from navigating at breakneck speed down a long winding road. For many years when I would get to this point, one single seagull would be waiting there for any scavenger treats we might offer. I was convinced it was the same seagull every time and took to calling him Livingston. Livingston was waiting for us. After he was fed his toll for continuing our journey, we crowded into our minibus and headed on.

There was only Adam and the driver on the bus with the women. I was at the front of the bus and could hear Adam's laughter at the back. I adored him. He was my bro, my knight in shining armor, my heart friend. The sudden way we had taken to each other carried on into the journey. I loved watching his awe as he discovered his own land. He was so much fun, taking care of everything in a gallant yet boyish way.

I loved curling up with him at night. He was a strange spirit like me. We were like the animals that curled up together at night for warmth and companionship and much much more that is not understood by most human beings. It was soon apparent to everyone on the trip that our connection was unique.

The journey to the ferry opposite the Blaskets was so filled with rich scenery; we hardly realized we were already there. We piled out of the bus at the top of the hill that sloped down to the ferry. Adam and Aidan gathered up three hundred pound Barbara between them, moving slowly down the steep incline to the ferry, helping her watch her footing. The sea was a bit choppy, which unnerved a few of our 'questors' as they saw that the ferry was smaller than they realized. Finally ensconced on the boat, we headed to the largest island.

Con had gone back to Dingle. We arrived on the Great Island early in the morning so we had plenty of time. You cannot get lost on the island. There is a path that settles across the high spine of the island that Diane, my best friend, who was also on the trip, headed out for. Others stayed close to where we landed.

There were small paths on the landing side of the island that most people meandered toward, 'getting their legs' as they explored an abandoned village that was built on the side of the steep hill. Adam and Aidan took their time walking Barbara up toward the top of the hill to the shop which served hot tea, soup, and sandwiches. Barbara settled. Adam and I took off for the path that led down to the beach and the sea.

Ever since we had landed, I had started to feel connected to something wild and powerful. I had no idea what it was, but it was what had me want to go down to the beach. We got to the beach after a half hour walk. Even though the sun was out and the wind was still, something felt threatening. There were four 'boys' that were on the island managing the tourists coming on and off the boat and a couple more manning the shop. I had noticed them looking toward the north.

Navigating my way down the sandy path, I had not looked up. When I got to the beach and looked up, there in the northern sky was a wall of black, far away for now, but it would not be far away at all if the wind picked up. Rain can be a fierce adversary in Ireland when it whips up from the north. The islands and shorelines of Ireland can get quite a thrashing. I could feel it coming.

I have never been able to successfully write what it is like for me when the netherworlds and I merge. I shift into an elemental being who has known the forces of life through all eternity and has, before becoming human, been a guardian of the creatures of this earth. It is not only a memory. I can shift into it without thought much like someone can swim without thought after walking on land.

I felt a rage roaring toward us, a dark power taking its territory back from the upstart humans who had lost contact with the fiery, windy, watery, heaving earth they belonged to. I felt the years of abuse the sea creatures and their home, the sea, had endured as human scavengers destroyed life with no thought. I felt fear.

I knew the storm was heading straight for us and I knew I had to do something. I looked in front of me in the dark cold waters of the sea and saw a single thousand pound sea lion and her cub. I instantly knew what to do. I had to swim out to them.

I sensed in the deepest part of myself that if I could bond with the sea lion and her cub, the rage coming at us might realize that there were humans who wanted to belong again with the sea and with the creatures they had forgotten. I knew I had to swim out there where a sea lion would, without a moment's concern, kill me to protect her cub. I also knew that something beyond the norm was up. Somehow we had, in our Quest, summoned the forces on behalf of humanity and we, or at least I, needed to make peace.

I was explaining all this to Adam as I stripped down to my underwear and bra. He was a strong swimmer who would come save me if I needed him to. He never said a word. He walked out into the water with me. Luckily for me, the sea lioness was very near the shore... as if she knew. The shock of the cold passed as I filled with the purpose before me. Mostly, I floated toward her on my back, the tide supporting my drift. I knew not to move my arms any more than I had to.

Within seconds, the newborn pup, about half my size and a fourth my weight came near me. I floated on my back, feeling the alarmed mother coming my way too. Sea lions are not the sweet cute little black seals you see crowding the San Francisco Bay. Sea lions are mean when they want to be.

I felt her primitive protection gather and I felt my terror all in the same moment. Then I surrendered. I surrendered to the possibility that we could move beyond my fear and her need to protect her young.

I surrendered to my inner knowing that if we made contact and I was allowed to survive, the storm would reduce its rage to maybe only a small grumble. I floated, feeling the pup come up to me and the mother circling only a few feet away. I didn't move. I was so grateful I was born to float. My dad could float too. He once sat upright in the Red Sea, holding an umbrella, and reading a newspaper until he finished it.

I felt a push against me. Then, without warning, the pup launched itself onto my belly. I sank. The ocean came over me so fast I sucked in the seawater and came up sputtering and coughing, violently flailing my arms and legs to stay on the surface. I didn't know it at the time, but Adam, forcing himself to trust me as he watched from the shore, was highly agitated and wondering whether or not he needed to come get me.

When I opened my eyes, I expected either to have the mother in my face, which would not be a good thing or both the mother and her infant long gone.

What I did not expect to find was the two of them watching me at a polite distance. They began to swim around me and up to me, recognizing my frailty, keeping their distance. I began to dog paddle with them, gauging the sea lioness's length, so I didn't make a fatal error.

When I floated on my back, again feeling into the storm, I could feel 'surprise'. That is the only word for it. The forces of storm felt surprised. I didn't know what would happen now, but the sea lion, her pup and I had connected. And in that connection, we had created a new possibility of another way of being for human creatures and the other creatures of our shared planet.

I smiled at Adam on the shore and waved, resting a minute before I made my way back to the beach.

I suddenly saw one of 'the boys' running across the hill toward the path down to the beach, and the moment I saw him, I heard Con yelling in my head, *"Find them!!"* I knew the 'them' was not only Adam and me, but my friend Diane who also loved to merge with the elements and the forces and disappear from view.

Realizing I needed to swim in, I didn't notice that the pup had come right up to me until I felt it nuzzle my side. I wasn't about to move even if Con called out the army. I lay there, the baby lying against me and the mother circling us in quiet attendance. I let the warm salt water of my tears merge with the cold salt of the ocean. I waited until they swam away.

Adam swam out to help me onto the beach just as one of 'the boys' made it to the beach. *"We gotta get off the island! A huge storm is coming! We aren't safe here! The boatmen are only going to wait another half hour before they go back to Dingle!!"*

As he and Adam were trying to dress my frigid and salt-sticky body, I tried to explain that we were okay. Everything was going to be okay.

But he wasn't having it. So off we went, at a much faster pace than I was ready for. I was breathing heavily and thought my lungs were going to explode, but was grateful the pace was warming my body.

I saw Con surfacing the ridge coming toward us like a smoking gun. I idiotically thought, *"Oh! He is back from Dingle."* It was clear he was over the top. I knew better than to try to explain to him that I had just swum with a sea lion and her mother and that now everything would be okay.

I learned, as he fumed at me, that he had had to, *"WALK OVER HALF THE BLOODY ISLAND TO FIND DI-ANE!" "AND...WHERE IN THE HELL HAVE YOU BEEN?! THE BOATS ARE ABOUT TO LEAVE US...WE COULD BE STRANDED HERE IN THE STORM!!!!!!!!!!!!" %*!# & ETC AND SO ON!!!!!!!!!!!!!!!"*

'The boys' had left the pile of tents inside the shop to have enough room to get all of us on the last remaining boat that waited for us. After I was practically thrown onboard, we headed for Dingle Bay, bypassing the ferry landing we had left from. The boatmen were concerned that if the storm started to move in, the waves would keep us from landing.

Con was furious and ignoring me completely. He had arranged for us to spend another night in the B&B we had been in the night before. I didn't say a word. As we landed, the rest of the participants were waiting for us as silent as lambs, concerned one wrong word would lead to our slaughter.

Deposited in our B&B, relieved to be away from the tall fiery furnace of Con, we all went to bed.

I never lock my door in the B&B's. For one thing, when I do I can't seem to get them unlocked. I had told everyone to sleep in. Adam was down the hall showering the next morning when Con burst into my room looking like he had never been to bed, which he hadn't.

"What did you do?" he screamed. *"What did you do?"* I just had to let him shout that phrase repeatedly until he was spent. I wasn't sure what he was talking about. *"The storm never hit! It was headed right for us!!!! DO YOU UNDERSTAND!!! It was headed right for us! It turned and headed out to sea! A northerly storm! They don't do that!!!"*

Adam came into the room and sat in a chair by the bed as Con sat on the edge of the bed next to me.

I began to explain what had happened. I watched as Con took it all in. Then he whispered, *"We went over this morning to get the tents. They were all gone. Nobody else was on the island. We were the last boat out."*

He shook his head from side to side, *"I know… I know… I didn't listen."*

"Please tell me, what were you listening to?" He said.

He wanted to learn. So I talked and he listened.

From that day on, Con would be by my side, no longer running into town, no longer leaving me to 'the boys', but by my side, not only listening for what I was listening to, but sharing what he was listening to also.

"Many a year was I
Perched out upon the sea
The waves would wash my tears,
The wind, my memory"

'Skellig'
—Loreena McKennitt

chapter twenty-eight

The Skellig Michael

The next day, we were scheduled to go to Skellig Michael. It was Barbara, our robust African songstress' birthday.

One of the most beautiful things about the trips is that everyone can go. Once we had an elderly woman, Pat, whose legs were rigid, strapped in braces. We would stay near her, but never treated her any differently than anyone else. One day, we were working our way through a mushy landscape toward a rough-hewn wooden fence. We were going to have to climb over it to get to the stone circle that lay on the tree-shorn ridge beyond. Everybody balked. The bare wood looked a heyday for splinters; the fence, though substantial, did not look like it was designed for climbing.

Pat, in her late 60's, hauled herself up to the fence and ordered us to support her as she literally threw herself across and over. No one complained after that. Off we went to a remarkable site… a line of stones stood like silent sentinels facing the Atlantic Ocean, overlooking a 200 foot cliff.

The same was true for Barbara. Corpulent, Barbara had a heart condition. We never babied her or stopped her from anything she wanted to do. Yet we always made sure we created an environment where she could win with her choices.

The quests I created were designed to achieve many things. Reconnecting to the land that still remembers us in places like Ireland is one. That reconnection alone changes the quality of a life. Once a woman in her early forties Becky, who was married to an Olympic coach, came on the trip. Becky loved Ireland, and felt at home for the first time in her life. In the USA, she lived in a fine, elegant house and spent her days chauffeuring her kids and making sure her home was properly attired for the lifestyle they maintained. Soon after coming back from her trip, she called me crying. I don't think she knew if it was from joy or from sadness.

"What have you done?" she cried. *"I am packing food in a picnic basket, picking my kids up from school and taking them to the park to have dinner. I can't stay inside. I need the trees and nature all the time now. My family thinks I have gone a little nuts!"*

I reassured her that it was like that in the beginning. If you had been estranged from what you are fundamentally a part of, and the connection is restored, you could get a little nutty.

Even though the family wondered if she was a little nuts, her husband Todd, an extreme athlete, came on the next trip with us. At the beginning of his trip, he could not calm down and was agitated like a stallion, chomping at the bit.

I finally said to Con, *"Wear him down! None of us can keep up with him!"* The next thing I knew, at lunchtime Con and Todd were running up a rather impressive grassy-sloped mountain in front of us. We had our lunch outside and watched as Todd and Con ran across the top of the mountain. Finally, Con came back down and we watched Todd 'take the mountain' for another three hours until dusk. After that adrenalin surge, Todd calmed down, perhaps for the first time in his life. Simply calm, simply present, with nothing added and available to whatever came his way.

After our great Blasket Island fiasco, we went back to the Blasket Ferry to take a boat to the Skelligs. That day, the seamen said they had never seen the ocean so calm in twenty years or more. The water was like glass. You could see the sky painted on the surface of the water. Glistening sparkles rose from the ocean floor, creating a kaleidoscope of colors. It was so spellbinding we delayed our trip for a half hour just to watch.

"This is the way of magic!" I would say over and over again. One can only know magic by experiencing it. For everyone, it was obvious that the day before when the storm disappeared, something profound had occurred. The sky, the ocean, and the land were honoring that. We also were aware that the elements and forces had that day created a moment for us.

We finally took off for the Skellig Michaels, which jut up out of the sea about twelve kilometers from the mainland coast. You can only get there by boat, and often cannot get there at all. They are situated in one of the fiercest weather areas in all of Ireland.

But not that day. We glided across our ocean mirror transfixed by the stillness. The earth was so silent you could hear your own breath. No one said a word. Opened up into the awareness of connection, we all lived and breathed the appreciation of the extraordinary that lived in that moment.

The boatmen from Valencia, there to take us off the boat, were startled to see us coming in from the Blasket dock. They were Irish, 'green with envy' that we had been able to come that way.

Barbara was the first off the boat. She loved the attention when all the men helped her off the ferry onto the dock. The dock overhung the usually choppy seas, protecting the passengers from being thrown into the water as they disembarked.

We came ashore with smooth grace. Several boats were coming in at once, taking advantage of the calm sea. Our boat was the first one in. Our group headed for the stone walkway that coiled around the side of the jagged craggy rock island, a snake-like presence tangled amidst frozen grey spikes of liquid stone poking out everywhere.

We found a place for Barbara to sit, a stone bench overlooking the ocean with a panoramic view of western Ireland. We were about to ascend over a hundred stone steps to an abandoned monastery where hundreds of years ago monks had lived. They had never left the island, living off the seabirds and fish that they caught. When we got to the top of the stone steps, we would be able to see the remnants of small gardens where they had grown potatoes to supplement their diet.

Adam and Con walked me up the steps, one incredibly steep step at a time, slowly moving toward the top. One thing I learned from Con, which I still do to this day, was to connect into another's energy field. Both Adam and Con were strong virile men, and when I connected into their field, I had more than enough energy to keep going. They held onto me, and I moved as if I were a part of them.

Everyone else was up long before I was, but it didn't matter. We all had become aware of each other and what was real and authentic for each of us. No judgment or prejudice marred our journey together now. As I approached the walled-in monastery, I was shocked that anyone could have lived there. The areas for sleeping were stone boxes that a large dog would fit into. There were lots of flat tilted surfaces to collect the rain that became their drinking water. Even though the austerity of this abandoned monastery was severe, the view was spectacular!

The smaller Skellig was clear today, not fogged in as it usually was. The jutting rocky island was covered with numerous varieties of birds, both islands being nature sanctuaries. The Little Skellig, however, had puffins, which look like chubby black and white parrots with thick orange beaks. When I arrived, everyone was looking over at the little island crowded with puffins, oooing and awwwing at them.

Walking the stone-carved monastery took me back in time to the rugged life of the monks. Founded in the seventh century, for about six hundred years the monastery housed twelve monks and an abbot. The island was basically un-inhabitable, with the exception of the tiny pinnacle at the top. Their devotion to God drove them to this isolated spot to seek oneness by living an austere life under the direst conditions.

Time and time again, Vikings raided the island and slaugh-tered them. The storms were particularly violent, since there was nothing in the way to stop the tempests as they swept across the sea. Now here we were, tourists, having experi-enced none of what the monks went through, looking at the ingenuity those human beings brought to their choices. That in itself was a 'learning'.

I leaned over the stone wall to see if I could see Barbara where she sat, many feet below us. I called everyone over to the edge of the cliff to sing her happy birthday. Thirty voices raised in song cascaded on the wind, down the green slope with the jagged rocks. As we finished, Barbara replied to us by singing an old spiritual I had learned years before about the majesty of creation and how we were blessed to be created, "How Great Thou Art".

Most of the boats had unloaded by now, and people gath-ered around Barbara, listening with awe to this large buxom cinnamon-skinned troubadour, singing the ways of Spirit. She ended to heartfelt applause and people crowding around her, asking who she was and what she was doing there.

By the time we got back down, she had names and addresses of folks from several countries to write to when she got home. The day had remained still, and we made our way back to the Blasket dock.

I asked the ferryman if we could travel with him back to Dingle. I felt that Barbara was spent from all the exertion and wanted to make sure she was not any more stressed than necessary. The man agreed, and we set off around the impressive and completely uninhabited green countryside toward Dingle Bay.

We were almost to the Bay when Barbara, facing me with her back to the water said, *"I just wish I could see Fungi... then my birthday would be perfect."* She had just uttered 'Fungi' when he leapt up into the air, a foot above her head and landed with such a splash that she was completely soaked.

She spun around just as Fungi came right up in front of her, no more than four feet away. She shrieked as he flipped and soaked her again. The boat stopped and the men kept their distance, understanding that this show was not for them. Again and again, with Barbara clapping her hands, laughing and sobbing in between exclamations of glee, Fungi jumped, flipped, and slapped the water, dousing her.

Celebration complete, Fungi went out in front, leading us into Dingle Bay. Barbara sat in front watching him as we made our way to shore.

"Ring forts of rock
The magic of the druids
Tombs of kings
In golden Ireland"

Clannad
—Banba Oir Lyrics

CHAPTER TWENTY-NINE

The Ringfort

It rains in Ireland. I know people know that, but you never realize what the words, 'it rains in Ireland' really mean until you are there when it rains. There are several terms for rain in Ireland. There is 'soft rain' which is mostly what we have in the United States. This is rain where, if we didn't use an umbrella, we would get drenched.

Then there is 'pissin' rain. That is something we don't get very often in the USA. 'Pissin' rain is a deluge, a blinding torrential flood coming from the sky, a 'clammy moisture' pouring into the marrow of your bones, making your clothes so sopping wet that 'warm' is impossible.

I found that the weather of Ireland moved with the emotions of the people on our quests. Often when the weather forecast predicted rain, if our spirits were high, the rain backed off and brilliant serrated orange and red sky-art plumbed the heavens.

The five years I walked the land before I brought people here, if I saw a rain storm coming toward me, I would let myself move into whatever deep emotions I was present to and weep with any grief I had for my life, for the planet, or for human kind. When I was complete, the rain would dissipate. I can listen and communicate with the weather even to this day.

On one particular quest, the majority of people came weathering personal storms, so it was no accident that we traveled half the trip in 'pissin' rain.

After the first trip that Con and I did together, part of our private banter was about what each of us was 'listening to'. On this trip, Con got back at me for all the times I wouldn't explain myself and only asked him to 'listen'.

The night before, we had arrived at our lodging located in an isolated valley off the famed Ring of Kerry. After enduring another wet day, we peeled out of our soaked outer clothing, and huddled around a large peat-burning fireplace. Our waterlogged boots lined the hearth. To our dismay, we discovered the hot water heater was busted. We heated water on the cook stove for people to hand bathe. We struggled to stay awake until dinner was ready.

However our chef, 'Beloved Jim', was more than just a cook. He was a natural healer who knew the magical power of food and was ready for us. Each plate he served carried a color scheme of appearance, texture, and taste. Every morsel fed our bedraggled emotions as well as our weary spirits.

Before our meal, everyone was exhausted and longed for bed. Fortified by Jim's 'magical' food, we revived and gravitated to the fire. Curled up next to each other, we shared the stories of our day late into the night. Finally, satiated by each other's company, we went to bed.

At seven in the morning, when it was still dark outside, Con stormed into my room, woke me up, and ordered me out of bed. Groggy-eyed, I stared at him from under the duvet. Quite animated, he shouted me awake.

"We have to be on the bus in 20 minutes!"

I struggled up, my Irish bedding wrapped defensively around my naked body.

Fearing the inn was about to be washed away I stammered, *"Why do we have to get up exactly?"*

In radiant triumph, he looked at me and said, *"Because I'm listening."*

We had planned to go to a ringfort later that day. I was hoping for 'much later'. The ringfort where we were headed was known as Cathair na Stéige or Staigue. Ringforts were perfectly round stone citadels built during the chaotic period of the early Iron Age (800BC-400CE). Fortified with ten foot or higher walls, they were used both as defense as well as for Celtic ritual. Legend had it that they carried magic that protected the surrounding settlements.

I had planned on sleeping in and then seeing if the weather had cleared enough for us to go. However, now it didn't matter if the weather was clear. Con was clear. Something had motivated Con to get there much earlier than we planned. And so, reluctantly, I was clear it was time to go.

In western Ireland it often rained in the mornings and cleared up around noon. Getting up early in the morning did not seem good at all. Yet Con had said the magical words "I am listening", so we rushed breakfast, donned damp coats, and lined our wet boots with plastic bags and multiple socks. Con herded us onto the bus and we headed for the fort. The early morning sun hid behind the clouds, but as we neared the fort, the rain shifted from 'pissin' to 'soft'. The dreariness of the muddy downpour of the recent days had worn us down. So in any kind of rain, we were not 'happy campers'.

As we approached, we were startled to see a string of black SUVs lined up outside the fort. SUVs are not the cars of choice in Ireland. For a minute, I wondered if somehow the CIA and the President of the United States had decided to visit this obscure ringfort in the middle of nowhere.

Infused by a possible mystery, we unloaded. No one seemed to be bothered by our presence. As we entered the ringfort we could not miss the eight men standing in their full length black raincoats, legs wide, facing out, hands clasped behind their backs. Clearly bodyguards or secret service. Not something you expect to find in the west of Ireland.

When I come into an ancient site, I always take a moment and put my forehead onto it near the entrance. That way, I can go back in time and see the past events that happened and experience earlier worlds. So as I entered the fort, with half of it roped off by the bodies of large burly security guards, I went to the unguarded part and put my forehead against the stone wall.

Just as I started to transport back in time, I heard someone say, "Cead Mile Failte!" (In English, A Hundred Thousand Welcomes!) I raised my head and looked into the eyes of a young Irish man who was clearly psychic. There is a look to those of us who can truly see. We seem like we are standing somewhere other than the place you see us, being with something you cannot see.

"Are you Tantra?" he asked. He introduced himself as Richard Waterborn's friend, Liam. Richard had told Liam about me.

I said that yes, I was Tantra and asked him if he knew what they were doing. He said they were scientists who were measuring the quantum fields of feminine and masculine energy in ringforts. To the average person this may not seem like much, but it is. There is a heritage of worlds that have been forgotten. When you begin to understand energy, you begin to understand the consciousness we live, move, and exist within.

Rediscovering that the feminine quantum fields were life giving and life enhancing and the source of all life on the planet could be very disturbing to a male energy dominated world, but it could also begin to put things right. People once built their structures in communication with the earth so the earth could inform and protect them. The scientist that stood on one of the walkways inside the walls was out to prove it.

Liam asked if I wanted to meet him. I said yes.

He got permission and returned to show me through. As he began to usher me through the maze of bodyguards, Con attached himself to my back, and announced to the guards as we moved through, *"I am her bodyguard!"*

Con and I looked comical as we walked as one body up the stone steps built into the fort to where the scientist was. I watched as a metronome looking wand moved back and forth on an instrument and then at some point stopped. The man, a professor as well as a scientist, told me that they were measuring the quantum field in the fort. I asked him if I could touch the wand.

He said, *"This only measures quantum fields not people, but, sure, go ahead."* I put my hand close to the wand without actually touching it and it moved back and forth registering, registering, registering. The man was amazed. Con whispered into my ear, *"Well, that's a h__ of a calling card!"*

I found it quite satisfying to be recognized as carrying an energy field that went beyond my own humanness. I had always known that, but to prove it was great!

We listened to Professor Phil speak about things that went 'mostly' over our heads. Since Con had worked with people all over the world identifying Ireland's sacred sites, he offered to take the professor with us to some sights that hardly anyone knew about.

Offer accepted, we returned to our inn for our midday meal and readied for our unexpected afternoon outing. Everyone was happy. A connection had happened because Con had 'listened'.

In Ireland, something is always brewing: a storm, a cup of tea, an Irish yarn, or the next great mystery. Veils that conceal the deeper unifying patterns of our existence can open in a moment. If no one listens, they quietly close and no one ever knows they were there. When someone listens, the veils open and the ancient mysteries of living are revealed.

I would love to call The Irish Vision Quest the 'Listening until Listening Is Fulfilled' Quest or the 'Listening Until What Is To Be Heard Is Heard' Quest. Yet, even the way we string words together deflects our ability to comprehend the realm of 'listening'.

In essence, without 'listening', we cannot see. The same image of someone crying could be a loss or a victory...a broken heart or a divine inspiration.

'Listening' often occurs beyond words...where the cells and the soul meet.

The art of 'listening' is imperative during our present transitional times. The imagery of life is changing and confusion comes with that change. However 'listening until we can hear' whether in words, sounds, or silences is fundamental to the magic of our existence. How else can we know the direction of our lives? How else can we know what we are 'looking' for?

That is why the quests continue to be provided. Whether it is personal or universal, the seamless fabric of our earth is revealing fundamental connections that fulfilled human life so very long ago. We are being asked to 'listen' so we can recognize what there is for us to 'see'.

BOOK THREE

QUEST STORIES

"Central to the ancient Irish mind was the mythological world of the Tuatha Dé Danaan, the tribe that lived under the surface of the earth in Ireland; this myth has imbued the whole landscape with a numinous depth and presence."

Anam Cara
—John O'Donohue

CHAPTER THIRTY

The Tuatha Dé Danaan

"I am going to write this!"

"No, you aren't!"

"It is time to tell the people about you! There are other humans that can remember!"

"No way!" The long thin tail flipped past my eyes, snapping like a whip at the tip of my nose.

Floating above my head, the shimmering pixie made his point by buzzing his wings at a fierce rate of speed.

"You are going into the book," I persisted. *"You all started this*

that first day, when the magic tried to drag me out of my bedroom and into your realm!"

"Bother! Jumblewaps! And Gumsnips!" The pixie popped at nothing in particular. He slowed down his wings and his tail swayed down onto my chest. Following the tail, I found a tiny pixie, a skinnier version of my big toe standing on my big toe, staring at me.

At that same moment, sitting in my comfy armchair with my legs straight out on the matching footrest, I felt 'them'. 'Them' is my colloquial term for the realm of the Tuatha dé Danaan in Ireland. About all I can do, even after all these years, to identify these diverse forces and beings is to call them 'them'. 'They' gathered tight around my chair, bulbous energy beings with a sharp focus emanating from 'their' minds into mine.

"Why is the dog outside?" 'They' emanated at me. I had left Lily, my feisty black kelpie mix, tied on the porch rail outside the door.

"Okay, here we go," I thought, *"I know how this works. Pay to play."*

"Okay, I will go get the dog", I emanated back.

Slipping on a man's pair of black rubber sandals left outside Diane's shoe-free home, I shuffled over to 'the dog'. Better known to me as 'my dog'.

Diane stuck her head out the door and said, *"Oh! You want to write out here."*

While 'get the dog' was the only thing on my mind, I garbled out yes, no, maybe snippets of conversation and ended with *"Yes, I do."*

That's how it goes. You respond to what 'they' say and you end up where you didn't know you wanted to go!

I was outside on the deck, which had been drenched in a recent downpour. Diane handed me towels to dry the picnic table and bench. I wiped the table and spread out another towel for my writing pad, folded the big towel and sat down.

"This is my deal," I said, settling into the negotiations to get permission to write 'them' into my book. *"You keep the water from dripping onto my notebook and me, and I will continue this encounter."* I have always found it best to act like 'They' actually want to continue. They like that.

Lily always gets protective when the realms open up a gateway. Disturbed, she jumped up on top of the picnic table and curled against my left shoulder, pushing on me until I wrapped my arm around her to comfort her.

Or… since she was not stupid, she preferred lying on a soft dry towel over lying on a cold wet deck. One truly never knows.

However, since she had never jumped up on the picnic table or sat on my writing pad before in our many outings to the writing class, I was inclined to think she was a sentinel on point.

"Okay," I repeated again. That word 'okay' somehow took care of a multitude of *'here we go agains'*, *'what nows'*, and *'oh jeezes'*.

"I AM going to write the Tuatha Dé Danaan into the book! I am writing you into the section that tells the stories of the participants

and the guardians. They were humans whose lives you touched...and I might add, some of whom touched 'you'!"

My pen paused waiting for a big raindrop to plop on my writing pad, signaling 'their' disapproval. No raindrop. I felt 'them' going into the stories in this section, pulling the descriptions of what occurred out of my head.

Starting with the first story of C, who carried their realms in her creativity, I felt 'them' take in that she was the artist for the cover of the book. Then I felt 'them' miss Lucy. 'They' remembered James's tears. A pause...a tender moment for the Tuatha dé Danaan when a human lets them in.

In my next breath, I felt 'them' remember Sam and felt 'them' aim a bristling disgust at him for being so disrespectful. Then I felt 'them' move into Sam's present life and see how with his mate that event was part of what shaped their reverence and profound loyalty to 'sacred living'.

Then 'they' remembered Marilyn. As Marilyn's story came into their consciousness, adoration for 'their' human 'child' oozed into my mind.

"That went well," I thought, hoping they did not register my thought. I still never quite know if a remark might be too flippant and become grounds for a retort. The Tuatha dé Danaan have a real problem with flippant humans.

I looked around. Drops of water splashed all around me but none on me, the book, or the dog.

"Whew!"

Instantly, a fat water drop hit me on the ear and another on the top of my head, then kersplashed on Lily's black nose.

Do not take anything for granted!

One of the many rules you learn dealing with the realms.

At least, nothing landed on the writing pad.

Contrite, I shifted my mind so they could move into the section called 'The Guardians'. Their demeanor changed. Appreciation filled the air around me for how Lisa remembered, how Diane brought balance and harmony into her work, and for Jim's wise and elfin-like spirit.

Then I showed 'them' that Con and I were going to do another trip. 'They' cherish Con and consider him 'their' beloved friend. As for me, 'they' have a potpourri of relationships with me: willful child, ancient guardian, one of 'them', human deal-maker who is bound and determined to join the kingdoms again.

"*---pesky girl,*" They hiss and the rainwater slides down off the leaves onto me again. I am a 'child' to 'them'. My age at 64 is nothing compared to their age--billions of eons of time as we know it has passed since 'their' inception.

I hold my ground. "*Can I write you into the book? It's important. This is part of humans and the realms sharing the planet consciously again.*"

No response. 'They' fade back, only faintly perceivable now. "*It's okay,*" I think to myself, "*I am through the door.*"

Who are the Tuatha dé Danaan?

That question can never really be answered.

One way to experience the Tuatha dé Danaan is in reading this book. Every tale in the book is the realm of the Tuatha dé Danaan making themselves known to others and to me.

The Tuatha dé Danaan live in the dimensional realms of this planet and rarely enter into our third dimensional confinement of body, mind and spirit.

They are the realm of magic. These forces and elements were born from the life force energy of this earth. Their realms embody the ingenuity and frivolity of creation and are playful and fierce, always engaged in the balances and harmonics that feed the planet and sustain the Tuatha Dé's ability to appear in physical form.

In time past, other dynamics of existence reached our planet. In the beginning, the forces and beings that came, melded into the ecosystems of earth. They lived alongside the magic of the Tuatha dé Danaan and others across the earth, realizing the importance of those realms.

Then others came. Things didn't go too well after that. These invasive species combined the natural substances and energies of the planet in ways that went against the earth's intricate design. They disturbed the natural balance that had the earth be self-sustaining and self-generating and disrupted the harmonics that birthed life forms with amazing capacities.

The Tuatha dé Danaan tried to use their magic to stop them, but to no avail.

Realms of dissonance, born of the non-kindred beings, began to take over the earth. To survive, the Tuatha dé Danaan escaped into the dimensional fabric of the planet. The invasive beings could not follow.

The earthly elementals and planetary primal forces found places where they could, in unity with the planet, sustain and maintain the vital energies, the blood, sinew, and soul of life here. Ireland was one of those places.

The non-kindred beings sickened the planet and its creatures. Many original progeny of earth disappeared. Others stayed but forgot the ways of harmony and balance.

To this day, the Tuatha Dé remain faithful to their creation crafting portals and gateways into the haggard 3rd dimension. From there, they search for those who still carry the original DNA of earth's magic.

The participants and guardians on the Vision Quests were touched by the realms. They struggled with the limitation of what 'human' had become yet they embraced their experiences and shared the magic. Here are a few of their stories.

"Between my potential and the deep blue sea,
There's a rock and a diamond either side of me,
Between our potential and the break of day,
There is nothing at all in our way,
Nothing in our way."

'All that Hammering'

—Mary Black

chapter thirty-one

Quest Participants

How do we remember what we forgot if we don't know that we forgot? Especially if what we forgot is fundamental to what we are.

The Quest works in a natural way to have people remember.

The Irish, the land, and the sea make our job so simple. Take people out on the land and the sea, where they have an undeniable direct experience with the core of their existence. Then, surround them with the people who are bonded to their land.

The Quests to Ireland are that simple, and that simplicity created the most powerful transformations imaginable.

'The Hits'

∞ C ∞

Faery rings can capture you, and cubbyholes in hillsides can draw you into them, in Ireland. The deep hand of The Mother reaches out to you where the connections to her have not been lost.

Sometimes you are looking for them and sometimes you are not.

Once C, the artist who drew the cover for this book, was wandering the hillsides of southwest Ireland outside County Clare with me.

It was C's first trip to Ireland. She had always seen elementals and had drawn them as illustrations in newsletters I had sent out. She was an interesting mix. She looked like an elemental herself, yet she was an elfin person who worked as an expressive arts therapist with mentally ill patients at the Ohio State Psychiatric Hospital.

Being an angel in dire atmospheres was her calling. Yet this calling often left her drained, and though her soul was deeply rooted, the environments she walked into every day disillusioned her. She could hold the barbed souls of the incarcerated, with tenderness and compassion, using the gift of art to bring out the parts of them that they had never known. C gave them a way to relate to themselves with truth that had not been possible before. The system itself was the biggest problem for her elemental nature. Without meaning to, the system made everyone ill.

When I first met C, she was so frail that I had her sit beside me so I could hold her in the courses and classes I led. She would shake so hard I thought she would fly apart. Her elemental energy ran rampant in her physical body. She was truly more creature than human.

Now, she had come to Ireland.

I walked with her quite a distance while she made her way back into the skin of her own belonging. She wandered, picking up stones, touching the earth, and smelling the flowers. Entranced with the warm, moist day under a bright sky, I moseyed away from her, leaving her to walk on. Lost in my own wander, I didn't hear her at first.

"Tantra. Tantra, come here!"

I turned and looked back. C was sitting on a rock in the middle of a faery ring.

"I can't move."

Well, I knew that. I had walked into a faery ring below *Dún Aonghasa*, Dun Angus in English, on the Aran Islands. *Dún Aonghasa* was a still intact prehistoric fort with an altar on the cliff wall, overlooking a spectacular view.

That day at Dun Angus, I had walked back toward the road only to find myself standing in a small ring of stones about six feet in diameter. For a long time, it never occurred to me to leave the ring. Then when it did occur to me to step over the small stones, I couldn't think why I would want to do that. Finally, a young Irish couple saw me and walked over. The young man reached his hand in. *"Let me give you a hand out."* And that was that. I went on my way.

I had never been frozen, but C was. She was a statue with a moving mouth. I reached in to move her but she was stuck solid. I would have had to step in and lift her up and carry her out. And I knew better.

I sat down outside the ring. *"When you can move, I will help you out."*

Slowly and surely the connection faded. C, elated, rolled over on the ground, hugging the earth for a long time. Those deep moments of reconnection are unique for each person. I meandered away. She didn't need my hand. Whatever had occurred was done.

∽ LUCY ∽

On one of the later Quests, I had talked my friend Lucy into going with me on the trip. This wasn't easy with her busy schedule. I had invited her for several years, knowing that when she could go, she would. I had shared with her the 'hits' people had: Marilyn at Tara, myself at the different sites, and others. I am not too sure the idea of 'a hit' was that appealing to her. I always wondered if she thought I was stretching the truth a bit.

I told her often that I knew how loved she was by the planet. I so wanted her to have the direct relationship I did with the earth and her elemental world. I begged her to come to Ireland.

She finally came.

Lucy is a great companion and traveler, the world's best person to have along no matter where you are going or what you are doing.

She was perfect on the trip. Being Lucy, she was there for people. She shared her delight at the countryside and the vistas. She helped out whenever and wherever she could. She loved Con and the guides. She loved seeing me work.

Yet, nothing out of the ordinary had happened for her.

Then one day, Con took us for a walk up a mountainside. I had put everyone in meandering mode so that each person could do their own thing. The four guides spread out to keep watch. I came up from the back.

I watched Lucy. She was leaning against a boulder looking back behind me at the view. Abruptly, she flattened her body against the face of a boulder, closed her eyes and spread out her arms, a human cross. Liam, one of the guides, saw her the same minute I did. The ground came to the top of the large boulder to which Lucy was superglued. He squatted down above her and nodded to me. He would keep watch over her until the moment of connection, the 'hit', had passed.

I went on past her. She and I were not staying at the same B&B, and I knew the next time I saw her would be at dinner. This was her private moment with whatever she had merged with. I smiled, content she had been captured by The Mother.

I ended up getting really muddy that afternoon. I fell and started sliding down the slippery moss, when out of nowhere, Con's hand closed on my wrist and I was saved from a long rocky slide.

Before dinner, I drew myself a bath in the shared hallway bathroom, and was relaxing in the hot water. I had had to draw a bath twice, once simply to wash off the mud and again to soak.

All of a sudden, and completely without warning, the door flew open. Lucy burst into the small room with only a bathtub and toilet. She slammed herself down on the toilet, and shouted at me, *"I hate you! I hate you!"* She was so shaken. *"YOU WERE RIGHT!"*

Then she laughed and hugged me. She was still stunned that she had been plastered against a boulder for forty-five minutes, gone into a netherworld of connection that was, she exclaimed, *"... SIMPLY UNEXPLAINABLE!!!"*

Hugging me again, getting herself soaked with my bathwater, she stormed delightedly back out of the bathroom leaving the door open.

Several people had come into the hall to see what was happening. You know to keep your ears peeled for the next great adventure on the Quests.

Lucy long gone; there I was.

Door open.

Fully exposed to everyone in the hall.

A naked goddess in a tub.

... Naked in the face of yet another mystery.

∞ JAMES ∞

Ireland is for everyone. The strange power of the land can grab you when you least expect it. Once we had a very well-to-do man on the trip. No matter how casually he dressed, he still looked like he was wearing a business suit--uptight and tight lipped. He had come on the trip in the company of a woman with whom he was deeply in love.

We had all gone out to see Fungi that morning, but James had stayed behind. He wasn't interested in 'romping with an oversized fish!' After wiggling out of our wet suits, we lunched, and went back to our rooms to change. We gathered up James, and set off in our second home, our bus, for The Burren.

The Burren means 'great rock'. Covering about 96 square miles or 250 square kilometers, the Burren unfolded before us, replicating the vast stone highways of the Romans. Except this was not a highway; this was the work of Mother Nature. As we got closer, we saw that the limestone and dolomite karst landscape gave the impression of a gigantic quilt, heaved up in some places and completely flattened in others. There were many sinkholes and limestone caves there.

We went to a famous wedge tomb standing in the middle of a landscape of barren rock as far as the eye could see. Two stones on either side created a small burial casket out of slices of rock, with a cap stone that was the lid of this stony coffin. The surface of The Burren was covered with a network of field walls, hut circles, and many other signs that indicated human beings wanted to be there regardless of how barren it was. As villages formed, they wedged up against The Burren's rocky edge.

After a quick lunch at a roadside café, we headed for the Cliffs of Moher, *Aillte an Mhothair* in Irish, '*the cliffs of the ruin*', at the edge of The Burren. The cliffs rise 394 feet (120 meters) above the Atlantic Ocean at Hag's Head, then continue to ascend to 702 feet (214 meters) not far away from O'Brien's Tower. O'Brien's Tower is a round stone tower high up the cliffs built by Sir Cornelius O'Brien, a descendant of Ireland's High King Brian Buru. Sir O'Brien built the tower to impress female visitors. The view from the tower was completely impressive…a spectacular view of the haunting Aran Islands poking up in the sparkling Galway Bay below. The wild Maum Turk Mountains and the striking Twelve Pins of Connemara were visible in a way that cannot be seen from any other place.

I saw James standing on top of the tower and made my way up to him. He had his back to me. I waited until he turned around. Tears streamed down his face. He whispered, *"If Ireland can touch my heart, she can touch the heart of anyone."*

A year later I officiated at his wedding, and yes, they have lived happily ever after.

Trusting and Respecting the Kingdoms

∞ SAM & ELENA ∞

Many human beings think they are alone in the universe or that they are the only conscious beings on this planet. These are examples of the arrogance and stupidity that pisses off the elemental kingdoms.

Many of the beings of the earth and the cosmos still live in unity with the realms they belong to and in an interconnected harmony with each other. They expect all living beings to operate with grace, sensitivity, and respect.

Most humans, however, have forgotten how to operate like that.

Woven into the intricate fabric of Ireland is an elemental vigilance for balance that keeps their dimensional realms intact. One of the ways they stay balanced is by staying dimensionally separate from most human beings. They do not take kindly to tampering with that balance.

There are many areas of Ireland where the elemental realms are very strong. One of those areas is an old trail from Killarney. Much of the path is boardwalk going through tall, gold, swaying grasses, which Con refers to as 'Irish gold'. These fertile grasses live in constant moisture, seeping up from the many streams that lace the landscape covered over by the grasses, as well as gorsh, and the variegated greenery of assorted plants and bushes.

Red deer, with Mickey Mouse ears that twitched constantly like saucer-shaped radio antennae, poked their funny looking heads out of the tall grasses as the interlopers walked by on the wooden boardwalk in their territory.

We had a very special young couple on one of our Quests. The man, Sam, was madly in love with a younger woman Elena. She had come on the trip to discover if she wanted to spend the rest of her life with Sam. Sam was so love struck. He taught me a lot about loving another human being. The elementals taught him a lot about being respectful.

Nothing is more beautiful than the love struck, and nothing is more annoying. The adoring 'I only have eyes for you' includes not having eyes for anything else. Sam was both beautiful and exasperating like an adolescent bowled over by the adoration of his love.

Everywhere we went we had to deal with Sam focusing only on Elena.

The day before our Killarney walk, we hiked up a mossy, emerald green hill to look over striking cliffs that cascaded sharply down into the ocean, the sea foam springing two hundred feet upward, spraying us above. The cliffs were dotted with ledges that, at best, would hold a medium-sized bird nest.

Con and I were the last ones to get to the top. Testosterone surging, Sam was showing Elena how he could agilely drop over the side of the cliff onto one of these outcroppings and gingerly pop back up beside her on the edge. Everyone else was transfixed by Sam's antics, holding their breath, terrified he might not pop back up again.

Con and I just stood there staring, the words *'not again!'*

coursing mutually through our minds. Without shifting my gaze, Con already heading toward Sam, I whispered, *"Get him!"*

The last thing we needed was a love-struck American male drowning in the Irish Sea. Both Con and I knew it didn't take much for one of those small ledges to break off and plunge everything on it into the frothy, turbulent waves below.

I had barely spoken when Con swiftly reached the edge of the cliff as Sam disappeared over the side yet again. I saw Con lean down. When he stood up, he had Sam by his shirt, lifting him high in the air, holding him there, and then setting him on his feet right beside Elena. He spoke to Sam sternly, but it was clear it was to no avail.

When I got to breakfast the next morning, sure Sam had been deterred, I was disappointed. Sam was busy sitting Elena down, then rushing to get her breakfast, then tea, and then whatever he thought might suit her fancy.

"Holy Mother," I thought, *"Not again!"*

Now we were outside of Killarney, walking the boardwalk across the meadow grasses. Sam, talking at the same time Con was, expounded to his beloved his own version of the Irish countryside.

I wanted to strangle him.

I had never been on this walk, so I was not prepared. We left the boardwalk and stepped onto an ambling path that zigzagged along streams that fed into the meadow we had just left.

The roots of the trees created small underground burrows that nestled into the soft, gray mud of the streams. The silence was commanding. You could feel the otherworldly stillness. If you were aware, you were immediately conscious of the presences that resided there. We were clearly in a residential area for elementals… tranquil and at peace.

We had separated Elena and Sam while we were on the boardwalk. Perhaps to give me some rest, but certainly so everyone else on this Quest could have their own experience, uninterrupted by the love dance unfolding everywhere they turned.

Con, Elena, and a few other participants went up ahead. Sam was not pleased. We entered the canopy of trees sheltering the streams with petite multi-colored flowers spread across the banks by the path.

Straight away, Sam (who had dressed for a night on the town and certainly not for a hike) tapped my shoulder and said loudly and with great bravado, *"I don't believe in faeries!!!"*

Instantly the air changed. The entire area went on alert. One moment we were enjoying peace and tranquility, and the next moment the hairs on our arms and necks were standing up from an electric hostility. A rigidity, a tension, filled the landscape. "Predators!" was the silent whisper ricocheting from burrow to burrow slithering through the trees and across the ground.

I, very carefully, in a soft but stern voice, said to everyone but Sam, *"Get away from here! Get away from here now!"* Instinct had taken me over. I didn't care how outrageous I sounded.

I kept making people get away from Sam and from me. I

held Sam back and turned to speak to him. Without warning, he lobbed a rock aggressively into an opening in a nearby burrow. The sound of the whack echoed across the roots of the tree.

I was stunned and sent grief, shock, and apology out into the prepared-for-battle air as fast as I could.

Before I could grab Sam and get him out away from the trees (and believe me, not for his sake, but so the little ones could restore order), I heard a scream.

Sam went running. The scream clearly came from Elena.

I held still. I knew Con could handle whatever had occurred. I needed to sort out the peace and tranquility that had so unashamedly been disturbed.

I stood there alone. I knew not to move. Let them read my heart and touch my soul. The air was still electrified, crackling against my skin, the hairs standing straight like porcupine quills all over my body.

The ground no longer felt solid beneath my feet. I closed my eyes, surrendering to the hostile inquisition. I surrendered up the deepest part of me for examination.

Later, after what felt like hours, my hairs settled back into place on my arms. The air was quiet.

I could feel the peace and tranquility again, although there remained a hum of alertness now.

I walked on. After a few minutes, I could hear voices. Walking up a slight hill, I came upon everyone standing around. Con's red hair flew about his face as he shouted orders. Elena was on the ground and two people on the trip were binding her ankle with tape from Con's equally red backpack.

Sam was the one Con was shouting orders at. He was silent and deflated, rummaging through the soggy grass, looking for whatever Con had told him to find. Sighing, I resisted stating aloud that we were still a long way from the end of the hike.

Seeing me, several participants came over and pieced together the rest of the story.

Elena, Con, and a few others were walking together when abruptly and for no apparent reason Elena, (who was an accomplished dancer) fell down, spraining her ankle. They soberly realized that it was the same moment Sam had lobbed the stone.

I looked at Sam. He looked at me. Nothing more needed to be said.

Con recruited the humbled lover and two of the other guides to carry Elena to the end of the hike. The others and I went on ahead.

The elemental energy of Earth, and the forces that protect them, do not take kindly to being messed with. The Earth is designed for harmony and balance. Anything human beings do to disturb that will be corrected.

As for Sam and Elena? Picture Elena's foot in a cast, sweetly cushioned on a chair, with Sam at her beck and call. Love, devotion, and genuine caring, with the added benefit of learning to be in harmony with the rest of life, won them a lifetime together.

∞ MARILYN ∞

Marilyn had gone with the other participants to swim with Fungi during our trip in Dingle. I had not gone. This was one of the few days that I was running around making sure the plans for the end of the trip were in place. It wasn't until we all got back together for dinner and settled in for the night that I heard the remarkable story of Marilyn and Fungi.

I asked her to write it out for me so you could read it in her own words.

My Experience with Fungi

I wanted to experience swimming with a dolphin for my spiritual growth. I had read numerous spiritual books about how highly evolved dolphins are, and that being in their presence, one's consciousness can be raised. The opportunity to swim with a dolphin came while I was on a Vision Quest with Tantra Maat in Ireland.

Tantra said she swam with a dolphin named Fungi in the Black Sea in Ireland, right where we were doing the Vision Quest. She said that, if we wanted, we would also have the same opportunity to swim with Fungi. Without thinking twice, I signed up. My dream was about to become a reality.

But then... an overwhelming sense of fear took hold of me. I knew the origin of this fear. When I was about four years old, I almost drowned and now I feared swimming anywhere I couldn't touch the bottom. I learned to swim, but never developed the endurance to swim for more than five minutes at a time. Swimming with Fungi meant being in the ice cold black waters of Dingle Bay with no bottom to touch as a safety net. This experience turned into a huge challenge for me.

I discussed my fear with Tantra, and she said my safety would be covered. Now it was up to me to make the decision to go. I did opt to go, if for no other reason, than to try and release my fear of drowning. The morning of the swim, everyone had to put on a wetsuit, which took me over an hour to get into. The weather that day was dark with storm clouds overhead. I'm thinking, *"Great, not only is the water black, now the sky is also black!"* I was terrified.

We boarded the boat and motored out to the area where Fungi usually swam. We couldn't see Fungi, so a man went out in a dingy and rattled a big chain. We were told that if Fungi heard the sound of the chain, he would follow it and the man in the dingy would lead Fungi to our group. Meanwhile, we were told to get into the water to greet Fungi. This was the point of no return for me. I had to either climb down the ladder and get into the water, or refuse to allow myself this experience and stay on the boat.

I decided to go for it, but I stayed back and ended up the very last person to get into the water. Before everyone left the boat, we were given a snorkel to use, a learning curve I didn't expect. I had never used a snorkel before and was given about a minute's worth of directions on how to use it.

I got to the bottom of the ladder, clinging for dear life on each rung. Now, at the end of ladder with the lower portion of my body in the blackest water I had ever seen, I put the snorkel in my mouth, let go of the ladder rung, and tried to paddle out to where the others in the group where waiting for Fungi.

I don't know how, but water got into the snorkel and I started to choke. Panic and terror overcame me. I was only a couple of feet away from the ladder of the boat, which someone not panicking would have gone back to--but not me. I saw a woman several feet away just hanging out in the water. The wet suit kept her in an upright, vertical position. I decided she was the one to save me, so I tried to swim over to her.

Choking and in complete fear of drowning, I managed to get over to her. I tried to wrap my arms over her shoulders, and through the choking, told her I needed some help. She seemed oblivious of my situation. I kept pushing down on her to keep from going under. Finally, she became aware of the situation, and either called or motioned for someone to come and help me. In the meantime, I was starting to hyperventilate and felt like I was going to pass out.

The next thing I knew, one of the men in the group, put his hands under my arms and gave me some support. He asked me what was the matter and all I could sputter out was *"I can't breathe."* While all this commotion with me was taking place, the man in the dingy was heading back to our group with Fungi rolling in and out of the water around the dingy. The man who was helping me motioned for the dingy to come and help. The dingy pulled alongside where I was, still trying to get my breath. I heard someone say, *"Take hold of the rim of the boat."* I was going to be taken back to the boat. I tried with everything in me to grab the rim of the dingy, but my strength and breath seemed to be dwindling. The guy who was holding me up also tried to lift me up enough to grip the rim but to no avail. The next thing I remember was feeling something hard under my feet pushing me up enough to grab the rim.

It all happened quickly, but I managed to grab the rim of the dingy and was taken back to the boat.

I was totally disappointed with myself. The fact that Fungi did swim for a short time amongst our group, and I had to stay on the boat, totally depressed me. I didn't get to swim with Fungi or overcome my fear of drowning. I learned later that Fungi was in the area where I was struggling to reach the rim of the dingy, and shortly after that, he had left the area not to return that day.

As I reflected on this experience, I realized that the hardness I felt under my feet that raised me up just a few inches to reach the rim of the dingy was Fungi. Dolphins have been known to come to the aid of someone experiencing trouble in the water. My dream of swimming with a dolphin was fulfilled more than I ever imagined.

Fungi is my hero!

"In your eyes faint as the singing of a lark
That somehow this black night
Feels warmer for the spark
Warmer for the spark
To hold us 'til the day
When fear will lose its grip
And heaven has its way
Heaven knows no frontiers
And I've seen heaven in your eyes"

'No Frontiers'
—Mary Black

CHAPTER THIRTY-TWO

The Guardians

I have always had trouble with the terms used in business such as 'team', 'staff', and 'board of directors'. The words themselves elicit such a disconnection from a living world, I cannot think that way.

The same was true of the people who were drawn to come on the Quests, not only as participants, but as facilitators of the environments within which the deeper kingdom could rise with ease and grace into the psyche of the participants. In the cold harsh world of separation, they could be called staff, co-leaders, guides, support team, chefs, and other words that have long ago lost their vibrancy. In truth, they were the guardians who had been guardians for many lifetimes. The Quests simply called them once more to their place in the scheme of things.

As with the participants that were called, the guardians also were called.

The Quests drew them together.

∞ LISA ∞

On another quest guided by Con, Lisa, 'in the world' a corporate consultant and therapist, came on the trip to support me and to add her own ancient harmonic. Con was taking us on a hike and Lisa and I decided to stay behind near one of the hundreds of villages that were abandoned during the famine. There were no roofs anymore in the once populated village and the stone walls had crumbled--weary from a weary time. The weeds had grown over the openings that had once served as windows, and the bog had taken over the fields that the farmers had once labored in. Con was taking the hardiest of the group up the mountain. It was too steep for Lisa and me to go and besides that, we felt drawn to stay near the debris of the village in homage to what had occurred there so long ago.

We went out to a clearing where there was only the soft moist grass that is so inviting to a weary traveler. We stretched out on our backs and fell asleep, grateful for the cool breeze and the warmth of the day. I had barely started my 'on my back' soft snoring when I heard Lisa whispering loudly, *"Tantra, don't move."*

I wasn't planning on moving. I was planning on sleeping. But something in the urgency of her voice had me open my eyes. I didn't move. I shifted my eyes left to where Lisa was stretched out, concerned that someone was hurting her, or given the urgency of her whisper, that a supernatural wild beast of some kind (since there were no actual wild beasts in Ireland), was about to devour her.

What I saw astonished me.

Holding as still as I could, I strained my eyes to see more clearly. Tiny bodies with wings hovered over Lisa's face. *"They're faeries..."* she whispered.

I knew that statement wasn't for me. She said it to herself, to acknowledge that a dream had come true. I saw the tears streaming down her face. I finally closed my eyes and let it be. They came for her not me.

Lisa and I did several trips together and usually shared a room. One night we were both in single beds that were high off the floor, the kind you need to have a footstool to get up onto. We were both on our backs again, only this time she had started her soft snore that I soon fell asleep to.

I dreamed vividly. Lisa and I were in another place and in another time in Ireland. We were in a canal hiding under a bridge with British soldiers marching across above us. We were holding a wounded Irish man who the British had placed a bounty on. We were keeping him quiet, which wasn't easy, given his wounds and his need to moan. After the soldiers had passed, I went ahead up the bank and pulled him as Lisa pushed him up the hill from behind. We were soaking wet.

We stopped and I held him in my arms. He took a few last breaths and then breathed no more. Lisa then came up beside me. Both of us held his thin gaunt body and cried. In the dream, we were sisters and holding the body of our brother who we had helped escape from a British prison. His wounds were lashes from a whip. He had been dying when we got to him.

Bitterness swelled in me and the dream shifted. In the next part of the dream Lisa and I were again in another dimension. This time we were dressed like tinkers, the gypsies of Ireland. They tinkered… mending pots, farm equipment, and other sundry things. For many years they lived in colorful wagons and now they live in caravans, which Americans call trailers, along the road. They still have their horses that they treasure and they still dance and sing.

We were modern day tinkers, dressed like janitors. We tripped over each other as we got out of a rusted old Econoline van. It reminded me of one of my favorite vehicles that I drove until I couldn't even get a puff out of its engine. We were giddy, losing our balance without falling, trying to carry a bucket of water, a mop and a long flat rake that I immediately stepped on. The handle flipped up and whacked me in the face.

It went on and on like that--a real Laurel and Hardy scenario. We were to clean this gigantic pavilion, with row upon row of lacquered wooden benches stretching across a hillside. From the elegant bleacher type benches in the pavilion, with a sound enhancing roof stretching over it, you faced rolling hillsides, lush and bright with green.

Finally we gave up, we couldn't make it happen. We fell down, we slammed into each other, we slid all the way down the pavilion when we mopped. I curled up under an archway and Lisa shouted at me to get working. I shouted, *"I may not be able to clean…..but I can…*

HOWLLLLLLLLLLLL!!!!!!!!!!!"

And with that, I let out a huge 'breaking the sound barrier' howl.

Then the scene shifted to the social room of the church I went to when I was young. Papa Kent, my minister was there and he looked at me, and the heavens opened up and angels flooded the sky. A booming orchestra started playing and at a deafening volume the voice of God sang out, *"It doesn't matter if you are sad or lonely, you belong to the one and only. It's over now!"*

I started laughing with relief. It didn't matter if I was in grief, klutzy, or if I howled. It didn't matter what I thought about myself because what loved me and what I was a part of had found me. The strife was over, the battle won. Sad or lonely, everything was okay now.

I laughed so hard, I fell out of bed. Thump!!! Crash!!!! Thud!!!!!!! My body slammed on the floor waking Lisa. Before Lisa could say a word, I started singing the song. *"It doesn't matter if you're sad or lonely, you belong to the one and only. It's over now!"*

Lisa started laughing and we laughed so hard that everyone came up and started laughing too!

On another journey to Achill Island, Lisa remembered the dragons and that her soul heritage still lived in their spirit.

This may sound strange, but when you remember, the memories fill the empty parts of your soul. You don't have to spew dragon breath or spend your life searching for faeries. You can go home and lead a very normal life. It will be fine. You will not forget.

∞DIANE∞

Sometimes I created problems on the trip though I didn't mean to. I had a tendency to go invisible. Con once drove around and around in a circular driveway looking for me when I was sitting right in front of him on a log. The other difficulty was sometimes something or someone needed my help. The purpose of the Quests was not to walk on top of the earth and its memories but to walk within them.

This is why I have a support person on the trips. I tend to what is wanted and needed innately, without thought. It is the 'without thought' that can be the problem. I go swimming with seals in dangerous waters or wander off, listening to the rhythms in the land.

That is what I am designed to do. The Mother tends the children. I tend The Mother. The Irish have a term for our more boring word 'babysitter'. The term is a 'minder'. I became a minder with The Mother. That relationship has not ceased.

I was thrilled when people who were close to me came on

the trips. One of my closest friends from Ohio, Diane, came on the early trips. She had a tendency to wander off too. She, like the other guardians, was woven into the fabric of the journey in her own special way. She paid attention and tended to me when things that were not so obvious to others were occurring.

We stopped at an unknown well along the Ring of Kerry. Michael, our guide, was explaining that wells and springs originated in the 'Otherworld'- that parallel dimension whose inhabitants have the power to control the natural forces of this world. From sources in the Otherworld, water flows into our world to fill springs or gush forth as rivers such as the Boyne and Shannon.

We couldn't drink from the well we had stopped at, so people moved on. I stayed behind, drawn to the well for a reason I did not know. I leaned over and peered down into the well. Without warning, the spirit of a small girl child leapt into my body. I stood up reeling, pale and weak. I turned to Michael and managed to stammer out, *"Get me to Diane!"*

I have such sympathy for the incongruity that Michael, Aidan, Liam, Con, and others dealt with on those early trips and such respect for how fast they responded to needs they didn't know how to meet or understand. Diane ran over, tending to me until we could get back to the B&B where we were staying.

I was not present. I was with a small child who had fallen into the well and drowned, long before the three foot wall had been built around it. She was looking for her mother. Diane, sheltering me, was listening to me as the small child

229

begged through me for her mother. In between the child's voice, I was telling Diane what had happened. True to her guardianship, she responded to ancient understandings, with no training. Only knowing was needed.

She got me into the shower and held me as I traveled beyond the veil looking for the child's mother. I found the mother. The mother found her child. The child left my body and all was well.

Dried off and dressed, we went down to eat. As we entered the dining room, four concerned men, four of my guardians, stood at the entrance waiting for us. Ah, the love of The Mother.

∞ JIM ∞

Each journey to Ireland was epic in its own fashion. Con led most of the trips but some of the smaller trips I led with a good friend and chef, Jim Dempsey. I met Jim soon after I came to Ireland. A gifted organic chef, Jim knew the relationship between food, the weather and the emotions. Once when I was suffering from a severe heartbreak, Jim took me up on the side of a mountain in County Wicklow below Dublin and cooked me potatoes, turnips, and parsnips. I was amazed how my heart stopped hurting. He explained to me that eating the roots of vegetables, roots you back into the earth again. The heart of the Mother can heal any heartache. It certainly was true that day.

Jim had been on several trips with me. He loved the outdoors. Dressed in brightly colored patterned pants and a simple shirt, he softened the heart of many a participant as he took them into his kitchen and showed them the beauty and wonder of food. On one of the last trips, we had leased a series of small cottages on Slea Head Drive near the Blaskets. The cottages sat on a narrow peninsula that stuck out far enough into the Atlantic Ocean that you could not see the land, the cottages barring the only view.

One of the participants lived in a suburb of Chicago that was wooded and closed in. The openness and exposure to the wild sea so affected her that I asked her if she needed to go stay at a B&B in Dingle. Most of us do not realize how completely adapted we are to our environments and when we are taken out of them, it can be shocking. Linda, bless her soul, stayed on until she could not only be comfortable in a closed-in world but also in an expanded one.

On that trip, it rained every single day, with a small breather in the morning and the evening. People had the choice of staying in or going out for our planned agenda. Every day they chose to go. Jim and I had our own way of communicating. Whatever I said, he understood. Mostly I never needed to say a thing. Nothing is more powerful than that.

One morning before we left, I said to him, *"Please feed us food tonight in a way that warms us up in every way."* He smiled his impish elemental grin and said *"Okay!"* Instructions given, off we went slogging the bog, and hiking the hills, with only a short reprieve of tea and scones in between.

We came back dripping with mud and water. Jim met us at the back door of the eating cottage and asked us not to come in for a half hour. We were crowding against the door by the time he opened it. The table, covered with white sheets, stretched across the room, decorated with blocks of peat with candles on them.

Red orange flames with green and blue tones danced inside bowls holding tiny chunks of peat. Jim and his partner Deb had gone to the seashore and gathered seaweed that day in the rain. The seaweed had been fried and oh wow! it looked so good. Before we ate, Jim said, *"No one feeds themselves. Everyone must feed each other."* And he added with a wicked smile, *"And only with your fingers!"*

Between the laughter and the erotic undertones of finger feeding each other, we were definitely warmed up. The delicious meal of fish and seaweed with grilled vegetables was followed by a decadent dessert of strawberries dipped in chocolate. Not only did we have the pleasure of feeding each other, we got the added bonus of licking the chocolate off of each other's fingers!

The evening ended with Eoin Duigan, a magical Irish musician, and his band, playing haunting Irish tunes. The most powerful tune, played on an Irish flute, comes from the tale of a man who often passed by a faery ring on the Blaskets where he could hear music. Finally, he brought a local flute player out to hear the melody. The flute player practiced and practiced until he could repeat the tune both in note and tenor.

When Eoin played it, you could feel the Tuatha dé Danaan, the children of the Goddess Dana, emerging from their exile and being drawn into the room. I have a photo I took while they were playing. The photograph completely captured the alive and otherworldly energy that was present that night.

Everyone went to bed late, intending to sleep in the next day as it was our last. A knock on my door woke me at dawn. The 'questors' crowded around my door, urging me to come out. Bundled in my coat, I was herded out the back door. Someone had their hands over my eyes. Once they had me positioned they moved their hands. I opened my eyes to the most magnificent sunrise I had ever seen. Bright oranges and blues streamed about the pale blue sky and the clouds merged colors and shape-shifted. The sky was clearly putting on a show for us. We all curled up together on the wet ground and watched, laughing and weeping.

We felt our unity with nature, and the bursting joy of knowing that the entire universe was acknowledging the courage, stamina, and determination we had demonstrated on the journey. We were being celebrated for who we had been for the past ten days that were anything but 'tourist postcard' perfect.

I know that if they had all whined and sniveled, and stayed dry and safe, that morning it would still have rained and the sky would still have been gloomy.

When you have been cajoled and bamboozled by the wonders of Ireland, you come away with a relationship to humor that allows you to see yourself from the point of view of the elementals and primal forces. You can howl at the shenanigans of what we put ourselves through as human beings. You can weep from remembering what you have forgotten. You can embrace yourself, knowing that you have returned.

The Guardians have gone their own ways now. Yet on the occasions when we meet, we shape-shift back into those who came to tend The Mother. We share. We laugh. We cry. We share the intimacy that can only happen in the deep awareness of our relationship to our Mother, The Earth.

"when it's over, it's never over
and when it's empty, it's never gone
i am in silence, gone from danger
far away is the forgotten one
i am headed from that distant lighthouse
i am twisting towards the sun
i wrap around me all your goodness
if i go that way, am i the only one?"

Who Do You Think I Am?
—Sinead Lohan

CHAPTER THIRTY-THREE

My Last Trip

I found out I had cancer July 2, 1997, eight years after I had begun frequenting what I now felt was my 'other country', Ireland.

I had gone to the doctor because I was rapidly gaining weight, only to find out that the lump I thought was fat was a very large tumor that had been eating my thyroid. All my nutrition was being consumed by the tumor. My body was starving.

235

I went into surgery the next day. The doctor told me that the tumor had spilled out into my blood stream. He told me I was terminal, and would be lucky if I lived three months.

At that moment, I was so grateful that I had lived my life as I had and made the choices I had made. Over the years of doing work in consciousness, I had gathered very talented and result-oriented healers around me. I had spent the day before the surgery planning my strategy to give my body the best chance it could have, to live. And live it did.

The first year was complicated by my immune system collapsing and by a car wreck that tore my ribs out of the thin muscle lining they inhabited, leaving me looking like I had been in a boxing match and had lost.

So I went into the second year, frail. I slept most of the time. Days blurred into weeks until mid year, when I began to feel the health of my body taking over again.

I had been out of work for two years. I had children to raise. Without the generous help of clients and friends, some who even went into debt to keep me and my children going, I have no idea what would have happened.

I remember the day I came home from surgery. I was sleeping around the clock and only waking up for brief moments. Every time I did, the television would be on, playing my favorite movies. One time I woke up long enough to hear my fifteen year old daughter, Liana say to her thirteen year old brother Aren, *"We have to make sure that when mom wakes up her favorite movies are on. Then her body will want to live."*

I really thought I was going to die. The vision I had of my

future life after my death was one of a smaller body with a man who was my spiritual partner, one of the new couples, who both had found their own way to their divinity, and shared a life within that.

There was nothing on the horizon that matched that vision when I found out about the cancer. I even told my daughter how excited I was that I could see the progress of my soul into my next life, and that I was ready to die. Now I know that I saw a transformation of my being that gave me my 'next life' in the years ahead without dying, but I did not know it then.

As I began to feel better, I was disturbed by my emotions. Even though I had experienced previous bouts of sadness, despair, and hopelessness like other people do, I had never had dark thoughts about myself and life. The thoughts I experienced after the cancer were vicious, vindictive, and violated my deepest cherished beliefs about people, myself, and life. The cancer may have left my body, but it was still embedded in my mind.

As I struggled with these dark emotions, one thought gave me hope. I knew I had to get to the Blasket Islands, the isolated group of islands off the Dingle Peninsula in Ireland. These stark and imposing islands have always been the place for me, and in my trips with others, the place to go to touch that part of us that does not know how to be alone. The fear of isolation runs so deep that we never recognize the gift of being alone with what we truly are.

I set off for Ireland, scheduled to work in Cork doing a couple of weeks of marathon consults. In between the two weeks, I took four days off and made my way west to the islands. I had called Con in Dingle, and he told me no one was going to the Blaskets that day, bad weather was coming in. But I went anyway, expecting to stand at the top of the stone ramp down to the boats and gaze over to the islands, begging them to release me from the torment of my mind.

When I arrived in Dingle, Patrick, the man at the top of the ramp who collects the money for the trips recognized me. The sky was a clear excited blue, no clouds anywhere. The water was so still.

Patrick was glad to see me. 'The boys' and I had shared many adventures bringing people over to the island, protecting them while they meandered the rough terrain and spongy bog of the land, and telling the hilarious stories that only the Irish can tell. I asked him if there was any way I could get to the island.

He said, *"Of course, for shu! The boats are running."* I explained that I wanted to spend the night but I had left my sleeping bag and tent in Cork, thinking I could not get over. What did he think? He immediately got on his walkie-talkie and called over to the hostel next door to the shop. 'The boys' stayed there to man the boats, and often young students stayed to run the shop.

With his thick Irish brogue, I could only understand a few phrases. *"Tantra's here... S'needs to face her demons... Have y' got a tent for her? She wants to be on the island alone w'herself... What d'ya think?"*

There was conversation on the other side of the walkie, with

Patrick bobbing his head up and down in agreement. As luck would have it, Irish luck, Diarmuid and one other of 'the boys' were the only people on the island for the evening. They were already planning to leave for the fortnight and go into Dingle. He had a tent for me, he said.

So one more time, I went down the steep path, walled on both sides by intricately fitted stones, a constant reminder of the rustic art of the ancient Irish. Feeling weak, I supported myself by using the wall as my prop.

That day I was so reminded of 'the boys' who of course, were not boys at all. Watching them, sea-weathered adventurers who raced up and down steep rough terrain and took their boats out on the unruly seas as easily as you and I get in the car to go to the grocery store, I felt restored. Their smooth grace and the confident strides on the rocking boats and rough terrain are as memorable as the extraordinary landscapes of the land and sea.

Once, when I had first started going over to the Blaskets, the tide was down. When the tide is down, they basically haul you over the side of the boat and down into a dingy that takes you to shore.

High tourist season, two boats were coming in at the same time. I was in the second boat watching as two of 'the boys' helped a huge woman in her late sixties over the side of the boat. They adjusted their weight and were holding her from moment to moment so strategically that she hardly realized it when she was over the side and into the small boat.

They exuded confidence, and even with twenty years plus

over them in age, I could not miss the primal energy that poured out of them, leaving the girls and older women like me, a little breathy around them. I loved them. They had been brilliant on the trips I had done. I loved their playfulness, the way they blended into the landscape. Their attention let us go places we could not have gone without them. Their comfort in supporting people negotiating all the different terrains was such a valuable part of the journey.

Today was for me. Their welcome warmed me. They kept to their own turf, but with a twinkle in their eyes. I told Diarmuid at the hostel I needed to walk the three miles to the back of the island before dark. He said he would put the tent up for me. I specified a small area down the coastline of the island overlooking the beach where the sea lions slept. Then I headed out across the ridge of the island with sheer drops on both sides and nothing to grab onto.

I have a phrase I use: *'between their ears'*. It means a state people are in when they do not notice anything around them. It doesn't matter how beautiful a place is, they can't see it. I was *'between my ears'* that day, and I knew it. I barely saw the white rippling that moved the water between the island and the land. I was in the fog of a vicious mind that was torturing me with every step.

It is a terrible thing to think ugly thoughts. Most people think it is normal and some actually believe those thoughts. Not me. Ever since I was three, I have been aware of another kind of mind that carries only the sanity of connection. I wanted that mind back.

I got to the back of the island and saw that the daylight

was receding faster than I had anticipated. Walking as fast as I could, I turned back until the hostel was in sight. From there, in the distance, I saw 'the boys' putting up my tent for the night. Confident I could get back in time, I turned facing toward the back of the island from where I had just come.

Yelling as loud as I could, I cried out, *"I don't know who you are or what you have done to me, but I want you to know that you can torture me all you want with these ugly thoughts, but they will never ever come out of my mouth. Nor will I ever operate as if they are the truth."*

I kept repeating it louder and louder.

Only a few times in my life have I felt the fierceness of my own energy. For a moment I felt feral, snarling at my mind, stuck in a trap that was not of its own making. I was shaking from the power of my own roar.

Then something happened. A tight-wired grid of energy burst in my skull. The force of the explosion was so strong that at first I thought I was having an aneurism. I sat down on the ground holding my forehead in my palms and closed my eyes. Behind my eyelids, light was forcing its way through what looked like black paper, tattering it, searing through it. It looked like a piece of burning paper, the scorched edges beginning to shrivel and blow away.

As the light burned through, a distinct sense of normal began. I opened my eyes, looked down at the ground, and the tunnel vision, I didn't even realize I had been looking through, was gone. I had a more panoramic experience of vision coming through my mind and through my eyes. The inner pressure of darkness was replaced with the inner stillness of soft light.

I was so grateful. I had evoked a healing through my own presence, my own power, my own truth. I had confronted what had me, and had said who I was and that I could not be turned. The powers of the heavens and the forces of the earth had eradicated what had sought to find fertile ground in my healing body. I had come to a place on this earth that was prepared for my deliverance.

My steps felt light and free as I hurried back to the hostel, just as the gray of night overcame the light of day. The clouds had not moved in and the dark was taking its time. 'The boys' were gone. The tent was put up, and around it they had woven a garland of dandelions, just like I used to do when I was a child. They knew. I knew they knew.

Everything pointed to the unspoken caring for a Mother who is the guardian of souls. Not me particularly, but the aspect of me that called them to remember more sometimes than I remembered myself. This ritual of leaving me on the island on my own, preparing my abode, was an ancient ritual, not just a tent, a sanctuary. I laughed when I crawled into the tent. Diarmuid had left a delicious plate of pasta, sautéed with lots of vegetables and potatoes. And beside the plate were quite a few six-packs of beer.

My bed wasn't a sleeping bag. My bed was a pile of duvets and pillows and wool throws. I pulled the mass of sleeping covers to the front of the tent and crawled in so I could watch the stars as long as possible before I fell asleep.

I zipped the door of the tent shut all around me, leaving only my head sticking out, in the late wind of the evening. I must have fallen asleep because when I woke the wind was gone and the sky was pitch-black, filled with sparkling crystals. The pinpoints of light were so vivid and felt so close, I was tempted to try to reach out and touch them. But the frigid pinch of cold on my nose discouraged any attempt to do that.

Over the years I had been traveling to Ireland, there was a particular dynamic that occurred when I state-shifted into the dimensional regions of Ireland. A green hue would color the air, as if a transparent green mist had somehow risen from the ground itself. While I was watching the stars, this green mist began to blur the sky. The effect only lasted a minute, and then the sharp detail of darkness backed off and the visibility around me was more like late day.

I turned my head to the right, and a mottled brown rabbit crouched within a foot of my face. I held very still, not wanting to frighten it. To my surprise, out from behind the ear of this bunny, a little fuzzy creature made of rabbit fur slid down to the ground and stared at me. The stare was mutual.

Something caught my eye beyond the bunny. I shifted only my eyes to see another rabbit with the same thing happening: a soft furry creature slid out on the ground and was staring at me. Sections of turf began to pop up as oddly-shaped creatures with green grass as their torso or twigs as their legs. They were everywhere, popping out of the ground, sitting down and staring at me. Enthralled, I thought, "This is better than Disneyland!"

Totally enjoying my dream, I continued to move only my eyes up the steep hill until I spied a grey thin donkey. A portion of the donkey's tail changed into a tail-hair creature that slipped to the ground and stood staring at me.

All of a sudden, I realized I wasn't dreaming. At the same moment that I realized I really was seeing them, they realized I really was seeing them. A kind of bizarre ruckus ensued. Some of them stuck their heads into the ground and somehow still looked through their legs at me. Others flattened out on the ground trying to be invisible. Somehow in this melee, humor vibrated through the ground. "Surely the ground cannot be laughing?" I thought.

I will never know. What I do know is that music did come out of the ground, a music reminiscent of fiddles and pipes. The creatures began dancing and jumping up in the air and plopping back down. They leap-frogged, bumped into each other, knocking each other over, did cartwheels and headstands, among other indescribable antics. There was clearly a celebration going on. They were thrilled that I could see them. I had not popped the lid of a single beer.

*In the midst of the reveling, they paused, some on one foot. Others stopped midway in the air. Still others stopped in mid-motion. A voice spoke with definite authority: **"That which is hidden from view will no longer be hidden from you."***

I must have drifted off to sleep shortly after those words, because I woke up to the tent collapsed on top of me. The wind had risen during the early morning and the tent had given way. I looked up and Con was fast-walking over the knoll of the hill toward me. It was the second time he had come to marshal me back to a boat. With the wind picking up, it was only a matter of time before the boats couldn't run. The boys were fast behind him, closing up the tent, running the supplies to the hostel, and herding me toward the boat.

The coolest thing was that I didn't feel like me. I felt like a unicorn. In truth, I simply knew I was a unicorn: silver horn, long white mane, dainty white polished hooves. I knew they didn't know and couldn't see me, but I knew. I covered the ground to the boat unencumbered by my weight, my strong muscular legs keeping up with Con's stride. He did turn around and look at me a couple of times, trying to sort out my sudden dexterity.

However, Con had been through so much with me by that time, he took it all in stride. I loved being on the boat. I trotted to the front where I could get the full effects of the elements. The wind blew my mane across my sleek white back as I shifted my torso from side to side, feeling my massive horse-body rolling with the choppy waves building in front of the storm that was on its way.

I didn't say anything. Con and the boys gave me space. We had learned each others' ways over the years we had been together.

My rental car was waiting for me at the top of the steep path. I headed up, so delighted. I had always had to pace myself. My lungs stopped working sometimes and I would have to stop to catch my breath.

Not today. Con said his goodbyes and hurried to get back to whatever he needed to get back to. I sashayed up the hill, snorting and clomping up the stones, besotted by the sound of my own hooves.

Just as I rounded the last curve, before the dirt path that took me to the parking area, I saw a woman sitting at the end on the wall. In an instant, I knew she was a retired school teacher. Her face had not seen much sun, both physically and emotionally. She limply held her sun hat in her hand, drooping with it. She was so resigned, so lifeless, drained from a life of boredom and fatigue.

Then she looked up and saw me, went wide-eyed and put her hand on her heart. I knew that she had seen through the veil, and even though she might not know what she saw, she had seen. The magic had touched her. I shape-shifted back into my human body just as I reached her. She reached out for me, and I reached back taking her into my arms.

This thin-bodied, retired school teacher cried out her loss of love and life, curling up in the stranger's arms that had brought her the magic. We stayed together a long time, watching the storm coming closer, holding hands. I told her stories of my exploits in Ireland. She laughed. She laughed the refreshing laugh of the newly reborn. I offered her a ride back to her B&B, but 'the boys' had already called a taxi. It was for the best. When you meet like that in another realm of reality, it is best to leave it in your memory unspoiled by getting to know each other in another more 'traditional' way.

I sensed I wouldn't be on a trip with Con again for awhile. His life would go in a different direction. Jim, my chef, too, had begun his own gourmet catering business and would no longer be free to roam the hillsides with me.

I sat in my car as the storm rolled in, glad for the intensity of it all. I would lead other trips. There would be other adventures, but they would be different for me. I knew that those two days on the Blaskets were the last of a series of initiations behind the veil of Ireland into the mysteries. Now I would watch as the veil of what normally lies hidden from view revealed itself to others and initiated them, as only the land of Ireland can do.

For Information About
THE IRISH VISION QUESTS
Email: theirishvisionquest@gmail.com
Or go to: www.metapoints.com under events

You Are Welcome To Write Tantra at

TANTRA MAAT
2945 Bell Road
Box 268
Auburn, CA 95603

TRIBUTES

Brendan O'Callaghan

My friend, you can indeed use the name of the Irish Spiritual Centre and my name if you wish. Anything that promotes the work of the Divine is alright with me. Fond memories of those days. God bless you, Brendan

Jim Dempsey

"Steeped in the incalculable romance of living, Tantra arrived in my life like a twin I had known forever. 'I know you from a place called 'Community'" was one of the first things she said to me. Her ability to move through this world and maintain her integrity in the face of a sacred sensitivity to the Earth is the most enduring memory I have of her. It would be many years before I would realise I was doing the same thing myself.

I grew up believing we were all 'like this'; and in a sense we are. She taught me that most Irish "turned themselves into granite" in order to survive in the face of the innate sensitivity that living in this land bestows upon us. She held that there is another way. It is rare to meet people who choose this way. The reality is that we ARE all like this, only some of us harden over a lifetime.

The option to stay soft and open is a challenging yet fulfilling path. We are alone on this path and the actions we take to maintain integrity on it are intensely personal. We must utilise the wisdom of every cell, of every organism to guide us. This is what I brought thru food. As a friend and mentor she showed me THAT to do it rather than HOW to do it. For me now, this was the true beauty of our relationship, a validation of my sentience that stood the tests of time.

Find your way. Maintain every cell as a whole, for each one counts. Even when you don't know what you are doing, you know what you are doing, a description of what became known to me as clairsentience many years later. She shines her divinity like no other."

In Love,
In Joy,
Jim Dempsey
www.naturalgourmet.ie and www.foodandhealing.ie

Con Moriarty

Tantra, reading your recall of the incredible adventures we shared in Ireland brings back rich memories and the re-connections we were honored to be part of. Thank you!

Reading it brings it all up so powerfully again.

Thank you for being part of my life.

I have missed you.

Love
Con Moriarty, Gap of Dunloe. Ireland
www.hiddenirelandtours.com

Richard Waterborn

Tantra,
Thank you for bringing back such wonderful memories of walking in the magic with you. The magic lives on!

Love, Richard
www.richardwaterborn.com

Diane Covington

Tantra,
It has been a joy to work on this book with you. I have lived the magic through the words and it has brought back such fond memories of my retreat there with John O'Donohue.

Blessings on the continued journey,

Diane Covington; editor
www.dianecovington.com

Margaret Sieger

I can just picture the crisp night air and the magical atmosphere and the exciting wonder of seeing the beings. The beautiful description of their antics and frolicking just brings the picture alive, and the hilarious description of them stopping their frolic in mid-step in their shock at realizing you could see them just makes me laugh and reaches right into my heart. But the whole book is fascinating and transformative. I love it!

Margaret Sieger; proofreader

Terrilyn Chance

Dearest Tantra,

Working on this book has proved to be a deeply moving personal journey into parts of myself that have been tucked away, buried and hidden for the majority of my life. The way the words and paragraphs moved in and out of me as I worked on the layout and design of your book were profound and magical. It was as if the book itself had life, presence and purpose, steering the very production process with grace and ease.

This project has re-introduced me to my own Irish roots, facilitating a "remembering" and a longing to explore and know those deeper parts of myself.

In gratitude,
Terrilyn Alice Chance; book design, layout and production
www.tachancedesign.com

TANTRA MAAT

Tantra Maat is a mystic, seer, facilitator, trainer, Interfaith minister, and a primal, spunky 64 year old who lives in an RV... that she loves... in Auburn, California. Tantra works both nationally and internationally, teaching her dynamic body of work called METApoints.

Tantra came to earth with a unique access to life. For many years, she could not describe that access or how life occurred for her. She only knew it was good and expanded beyond the human conversations she heard around her.

Almost 40 years ago, she began to sit with and "read" her friends, and when she did, something happened. After she spoke what she saw, they gained more ability to sustain a trust of themselves, of what they sensed or felt to be real. For longer and longer periods of time, they could sustain an innate sense of knowing their experiences, transcended beyond the boundaries of how the culture classified them. They began to hear, to experience, and to recognize who they were and what they came here for. It was time for Tantra to "do what she came here to do," voiced her friend, Sue.

Tantra left her employment in a mystical state, not even realizing why she had quit, knowing only that some great force had changed the course of her life. Within a few months, Tantra had a full schedule, simply by word of mouth, which continues to this day.

Tantra is a recognized cellular empath (which is one who has a direct relationship to the cellular resonance of the "other"). In this resonance is the truth of the other's authentic Being, what they truly came to earth for, and what they came to be with! In accessing this resonance, Tantra is able to see and speak into the other's current awareness. This untangles neuro-pathways that were scrambled from life experiences and interpretations, and puts them back on track, aligned with their own truth.

Tantra has spent the last 35 years growing into and distinguishing the beauty of what human beings are and contributing that, as a way of living, to her world and her clients. Now, she sees us standing on a new edge, where we are more capable of achieving fulfillment and creating a new norm.

CPSIA information can be obtained at www.ICGtesting.com
Printed in the USA
LVOW041007100113

315141LV00001B/271/P